CLAIMED BY WOLVES

A REVERSE HAREM SHIFTER ROMANCE

MOON CRESCENT CASINO
BOOK ONE

SARWAH CREED

ARYA KARIN

ABOUT ARYA KARIN

Arya Karin lives in the south and writes steamy romance and action.

Besides being crazy about reading and obsessed with all things romance, she likes to dance, sing, and spend time with her family.

Want to know more about Arya? Click here to go to her website- https://autho-raryakarin.blogspot.com/

Or sign up for her newsletter: http://eepurl.com/c7lTtr

ABOUT THE AUTHOR

Sarwah Creed is the Queen of comedy, the Empress of reverse harem, and the Mistress of jaw-dropping twists.

When she's not busy writing her Reverse Harem books that will leave you feeling hot and steamy, then you'll find her in the gym, running, or playing tennis with her kids.

Sarwah's books are available in English, German, Dutch, Spanish, French, and Italian.

She has a sweet tooth and can easily be bribed with chocolate and cupcakes.

If you're a new reader to Sarwah, don't hesitate to sign up for her newsletter and you'll receive a free book!

When you're reading her books, make sure to have a towel nearby because her stories are so steamy, that you'll need something to cool you down!

All social media links----https://linktr.ee/SarwahCreed

I've been sold to three wolf shifters.

After my husband lost big time at the casino, guess what the douche did? He sold me to the local pack as payment for his debt. Three owners, to be specific who look at me like they want to eat me. They are scorching hot, dangerous, and might very well be my undoing.

But I guess they can't be all bad… after all, they offered me a deal.

Stay with them for 30 days in the casino, and the debt will be paid off. But I'm no fool and know there's a catch. I just need to work out what that is and what exactly they want from me.

30 days.

I tell myself I can survive this, but it turns out I was right, and there are more secrets than I ever expected. Secrets that might very well keep me here longer than the deal we've made.

They insist they will claim me that I will

beg them to stay by the end. I laugh because clearly, they don't know me. I have every intention to prove them wrong, and then I'm leaving town and leaving my loser husband behind. I just hope I haven't taken on more than I can chew.

agua

What's a girl to do when she's stuck alone in a hotel suite?

Raid the mini bar?

Watch a movie or two?

Eat as much candy as she can from the mini bar?

Or even call room service?

I'd never had a phone in my room before. We had one in the diner and the house, but one all to myself felt like a luxury. I didn't realize how out of touch, I'd been with everything. My finger traced the silver vermeil on my wrist with so many different colors from blue topaz to orange sapphire. I didn't have jewelry any more, so it felt like such a precious gift. A gift from my husband, passed to him from his dead mother. She'd received it from his grandmother. I wished I could meet them.

Husband!

The thought of him brought a tingle inside of me. I'd left SmallHeath, the place where I'd lived all my life to come to Vegas with a man I'd only known for one week. Yes, it was crazy, but love is love, and Keith had captured my heart in such a small amount of time.

Keith's beat-up car broke down. We could only enter from the boot or we had to manually put the windows down, but it wasn't so bad. It managed to get us here and we'd driven two hundred miles, before the car finally gave up and we had to hitch-hike the rest of the way.

It was the most exciting and thrilling thing I'd ever done in my life. Well, besides driving to Vegas and getting married. Keith said he'd been on the way to Vegas to play in some underground poker game. He charmed me with his tall physique, emerald eyes, and dark hair. Everyone in SmallHeath looked the same, dark hair and matching eyes. I'd never seen eyes so dark before. They didn't look real, but I knew they were. I'd seen them on pictures and shows, though never in real life. And Keith was different. He was from out-of-town way down in New Orleans. He'd even been to New York, L.A., Chicago, so many cities I'd dreamed of going one day, and he promised to take me.

He drove a beat-up Ford, only possessed two suits, and was on the road all the time. He couldn't carry his whole wardrobe with him. Besides, he looked hot. No one in town wore a suit. Men either wore overalls or jeans. They tended to work in the farms, in the mountains chopping up wood, or making paper at the local factory.

"How about now?" I asked, my stomach clenching that he might just laugh at me. Here I was a stranger asking to go on a road trip with him. My dad would freak out. He'd always kept me stuck at home, but today he was on one of his many business trips. He couldn't stop me from leaving, not that I'd ever tried.

"How old are you?" Keith rubbed the

stubble on his chin as he looked me up and down.

"Old enough."

He raised an eyebrow at me. "Don't get me going to jail now, sweetheart."

"Twenty-five. I know I look younger than I am, but I promise I'm legal on all counts." I leaned against his car as he finished changing the tire.

"All right, Fagua." He stood and tossed the tire iron in the trunk. "I'll take you with me to Vegas. On the way, we can get to know each other."

We talked and goofed off the whole way. So when he asked me the truth or dare for the fourth time, I picked dare.

"Have you ever done anything crazy?" he asked.

I didn't want him to think I was a prude. The craziest thing I'd done in my life was jump in the car and get out of this town. "I thought I was doing a dare, not a truth."

"Right." He winked. "I dare you to marry me."

"Seriously?" My breath sped up, thinking I'd gotten more than I'd bargained for. No man had ever looked at me twice. I was Afi's daughter, the woman no man could go near without his permission, which was why I was the only one over twenty-one who had never been married. I went to high school, graduated, and just stayed. I knew no one outside of town, and as much as I was curious to find out what lay beyond the mountains which enclosed our town, I never had the funds to find out.

"Bet you never have done anything even close to this in your life."

Marry a man I just met? No way. But the thought of it thrilled me. Pa would be furious. What did he expect though? I was a grown woman whom he kept practically locked up at home in a small-dink town.

I worked in my parents' diner. This was my fate until Keith had come into town. I would carry on working there until one of the two eligible men in our town would ask for my hand in marriage. One of them was a drunk, and the other, let's just say, every girl he dated back in high school—and there weren't many— had a black eye while dating him.

So, I had the option of a woman beater or a drunk? Ma said beggars couldn't be choosers. I knew she was right, but I didn't want to break her heart and tell her I wanted out. I didn't want to have kids and run a diner, or the local paper factory dad owned, for the rest of my life. I wanted so much more. I needed to see the world before I settled down, and if so be it, one day return to SmallHeath, it would be before knowing what was outside town.

Our first stop was to the chapel to get married. Keith didn't have money to buy an official wedding ring, so we just used the Coke can ring. He said he would buy me one once he had his official win.

Our second stop was to the Moon Crescent Casino for him to get his big win. Everything felt so surreal like a dream whirlwind, and I hung on for the ride. Using Keith's phone, I snapped a photo of me and him smiling with a message we were married. Instantly, his phone rang, but I didn't answer.

After we checked into the hotel, Keith gave me a quick kiss.

"Make yourself at home, sweetheart. Whatever you want."

"I want you. It's our honeymoon."

My gaze shifted across the room. I'd never

stayed in a hotel before. Everything about this trip had been a new experience. I ran my fingers on the two-seater leather sofas opposite the bed. I'd squealed like a child the moment we'd walked into the room. Everything perfectly matched from the cream walls to the matching carpet which made me want to take my shoes off so I could sink my toes into the deep threads.

"Soon baby, soon. Let me go win our millions and then we'll fly to Paris or wherever the hell we want." He gave me another kiss.

After he'd gone, I checked out some movies on the TV. A small thunderstorm put off checking out the pool and hot tub. I had a smile on my face. I was a married woman now, not to the town drunk or receiving acts of violence from my husband. Someone I had chosen and not Pa. I felt like a woman, even if I was still a virgin.

The phone rang, and I raced to answer. No, more did I worry about what to do in the room, I was sure my husband was on the other side of the line.

"Hello?"

"Hey, it's Keith." He sounded out of breath.

"Hi. Are you ok—"

"Everything happened exactly like I said it would. Get ready. Wear the sexy black number you have, and we're going out to celebrate."

"Congratulations." I beamed into the phone. "I'll be downstairs in twenty minutes."

Keith hung up, and I did the same.

My hand trembled at the idea of everything falling into place. It was a strange habit I had, like most people who twitch or get nervous when they're nervous. I do the same thing, but when I'm happy, and excited like I am now. Sometimes, for some crazy reason, it can make the room shake, too. When I was younger it used to do that, but as an adult, I'd managed to keep it under control. Still, the pictures on the wall vibrated slightly. I had to keep my power under control, which meant my emotions, too. I inhaled and let my breath drag out, as Mahad had showed me to do one too many times, and then everything calmed down including my pounding heart.

Keith was my knight in shining armor. The way his lips curled as he smiled, and his eyes lit up, as if he would do anything for me, even though we hadn't known each other for long.

Besides, Ma and Pa hadn't known each other long before they'd gotten married. Pa's family had moved to the area. They wanted to get away from the hustle of the city, and they fell in love instantly. Which I reminded them of one of the numerous text messages they'd sent to Keith's cell.

I stood twisting my imaginary gold earrings, until I remembered that Keith had said that we had to sell them to buy gas on the way. They had been my most expensive possession. A gift from Ma on my twenty-first birthday.

I hesitated thinking about calling them all. I lifted the hotel suite phone, up and down a couple of times, before deciding it was best not to call Ma and Pa yet. Not until I had my wedding ring on and knew exactly how much Keith had won.

He'd sold my phone the moment we got here, so he could buy a suit and go to his game. He said to make sure he looked the part. He did as he left in a dark blue suit with a matching tie.

He looked the part, and I stared back at my reflection as my dark hair was tied up in a loose bun, and my matching dark eyes glowed. I hadn't been this happy in a long time. It was as if everything I'd ever wished for had come true from the moment Keith's car had broken down, and he'd stopped in our town.

I'd only eaten once since we'd gotten here. I never had a big appetite, but the plate of pancakes I had this morning lasted me this long as I ignored the rumbling sounds from my stomach. My dress didn't fit the same way it had when I graduated from high school. It was the only time I'd dressed up for a special occasion, apart from my wedding last night, and my best friend from high school, Rebecca's wedding four years ago. I didn't have a reason to have anything of luxury, because nothing really happened in town apart from weddings, which were few and far between, and funerals which occurred even less. I bought a dress in a color suited both occasions. Now, it hung on me, emphasizing once-full breasts that were slowly disappearing, and my jawline was starting to become drawn.

I picked up a purse Rebecca had given me as a parting gift, a gold one she had used at her wedding, and took a deep breath.

I was ready, and I didn't want to keep Keith waiting. I walked over to the door, but checked myself in the mirror one last time to ensure I looked perfect because I didn't want to disappoint him.

I smiled with satisfaction, as I hoped he would be as pleased with the effort I'd made.

As I swung open the door, there was a big man in front of it. So, big I gasped with shock at the surprise of seeing a man blocking my exit. He was super tall and muscular like a football player, with snow-white hair, sapphire eyes, and a smirk on his full lips. He looked like he'd stepped out of one of those fancy magazines I'd seen at the supermarket. He wore a tailor-made black suit and not at all like anyone back home.

"Yes?" I quivered as he stared at me.

"Fagua Strong?" He asked as he raised an eyebrow.

Two men standing behind him appeared, and the first thing I remembered was about Ray Hope from town. He said Keith had checked out and not paid his bill when he'd left the hotel. I paid after Keith said he must have forgotten and was keen to get to Vegas. Now an uneasy sensation tangled in my gut.

"Yes," I whispered, finding it hard to speak.

The frame of this man who must have been at least six-foot-four blocked my clear view of the other two. I backed away from the door into the suite and they followed, uninvited. What could I do against three men? I didn't have any pepper spray, and my throat closed.

I should have told him he was rude, and my husband was downstairs waiting for me, but every protest I had in mind stayed there. I found myself unable to speak as one of them had the bluest eyes I'd ever seen, with snow white hair. It was surreal, how the three biggest men I'd ever laid eyes on, all in matching black suits, from the shirts to their tie were crowded in my hotel room. I was too scared to look at their faces, as my eyes became fixated on their feet. Pa has big feet. He's a size eleven, but these guys must be like size thirteen, maybe fourteen. Damn, everything was huge about them and for some reason my eyes traced to their pants wondering if that was huge, too.

Stop it, you're a married woman! I thought to myself as the aroma of their forest smell took over the room. Yet, my heart hammered out of control, and I clutched my purse to my chest.

"We don't want to alarm you. There's no need to be afraid," the one with the white hair spoke. The crazy part was my heart started to slow down like part of me fully believed this stranger's words.

"We just want to talk."

"Yes," said the one at the back. He moved into the light as my gaze shifted in his direction, but then back to the one with white hair, who didn't feel like some kind of animal, because he had a soothing voice, unlike the other two.

"We're the Crescent brothers. I'm Winter, and these are my brothers, Sky and Husk. Keith sent us here to talk to you."

I shook my head, not quite believing what they were saying. "Keith? My husband?"

The three guys pushed into the room and I rushed backward. One stood between me and the door, while the other two moved to the windows.

Oh god, were they checking the room to make sure there were no escape routes for me?

I inched toward the hotel phone on the night-stand, trying not to be too obvious.

"Yes, your husband," Winter said.

"How long have you been married?" Husk demanded. I thought his name was Husk. I wasn't quite sure because Winter had said their names, but he didn't make it clear which one was Husk or Sky.

What weird names.

Shit, then my senses started working overtime.

The names.

Their frames.

Their scents.

It could only mean one thing, they were wolves!

"One night." My heart raced out of control again. As my gaze flashed to the door, I wondered if I could run out of here fast enough. I had a feeling they would catch me.

"One night," Husk chuckled, and the glow of his white teeth startled me.

"Yes. One night."

I threw my purse on the sofa, and the fear was in me, washed away as I drew nearer towards him.

"I told you to let me come alone. You two are never good at this type of thing," Winter said as he shook his head and stamped his foot. He had my attention, and the wolf I'd thought was the calm one made me quickly change my mind.

"You see, my brother finds it amusing how your so-called husband would get rid of you on the first night of marriage," Winter explained to me.

I didn't understand what he was talking about. I lifted my chin. "Keith just called and said I should meet him downstairs."

Husk, still laughing, said, "Go down and meet him then. We'll wait."

I grabbed my purse, thinking not only would I go down to meet him, but bring him back to the room and show these wolves my husband hadn't gotten rid of me. He wouldn't do that, even if we'd only known each other for a short time. He loved me. That was what he said as we'd gotten married. When we came up to the room he told me he wanted to be with me for the rest of his life. Unshed tears stung the back of my eyes as the reality of my thoughts started to feel like a dream.

No, I would show them all they were wrong.

Husk continued to laugh as I slammed the door shut. I had a feeling he had a good reason for laughing, the same as I had for wanting to cry right now.

CHAPTER 2

*W*inter

"Why do you always have to alienate everyone? I told you I would come up here and speak to her alone," I said to my brothers. They were both doing what they did best, ignoring my request and fucking everything up.

"We were curious, brother, and we wanted to see her. We wanted to know if she was as beautiful as we imagined. The seer told us she was the answer to survival. We had to see if it was true." Sky tore himself away from the window.

I know what he wanted to do. He wanted to get on the balcony and really freak her out. Show off his muscles and dive off the ledge to land unharmed nine floors below.

I hadn't even told her what had happened tonight. Some part of me knew she wouldn't be able to handle it with Husk's deep stare and Sky's weirdness. I love my two brothers, but when it comes to matters of the heart, they're as brutal, and as rough, as it comes.

Husk's idea of a pick-up-line is, "You, me tonight my place."

Sky's was a wink.

I'm the one who does all the negotiations, the one who doesn't scare away anyone we do business dealings with, because of the other two. Their wolf instincts always take over, and it goes bad. Every single time.

"I wonder if she felt it? I felt as if my insides were about to rip from the moment we entered the room. I couldn't speak. Everything was out of control, a weakness I never knew I possessed until now," Sky said as he tried to open the balcony.

"Fuck, Sky. You're not going out." Husk opened the nightstand drawer, moving stuff around before grunting and closing it back. "Remember the last time you did that. You nearly gave one of the cleaners a heart attack when you jumped off the damn roof."

"My wolf instinct wanted to take Fagua." He shook his head. "Claim her, so damn badly I could hardly speak. The only way to calm myself down is to fly."

Husk snorted. "You don't see me running around in the casino. You need to control yourself. Seriously, we don't need our secret coming out, and the way you've been reckless lately, it may just happen. But I do understand what you mean. I felt it too. Winter didn't. He was as calm as always, which reminds me..." He paused to pull out his cigar. There was a no-smoking policy, but we were the owners, and at times, we broke the rules. Husk could complain about Sky feeling the need to fly, but there was no doubt the smoking cigars kept Husk's wolf urges at bay.

He opened the door. Sky hesitated as he was about to join us outside, and then he went back inside the room. He went to the mini bar to pour himself a drink. I didn't know which was worse, his newfound love of drinking or flying over the casino?

"How long will you give Fagua downstairs before she figures it out?" Husk lit his cigar, taking a few puffs. He kicked up his cowboy boots onto the metal table. His smoke curled up into the night air. "We could be here all night, and we have work to do."

I nodded, "I know, but she needs time to process her loser husband who has done a runner and left her with his debt."

Sky said, "Good news. They never had sex."

I shook my head as Sky kept sniffing the sheets and concluding Fagua was a virgin. Their wedding may not be consummated, but Keith had his pleasure with her, even if it was in other ways. Filthy dog. We had a deal, and he had clearly stepped over the line, first by marrying her, and then bringing her here as his wife.

Sky only shifted around three months ago. He knew it was coming, but whereas Husk and I had shifted since we were teens. It took Sky a lot longer, and with it came gifts so strong he hadn't been able to control. A bottle of JD seemed to have become his new best friend.

"Go. Go talk to her. Before your brother drinks out the mini bar," Husk commanded.

He was the first to be born and loved to shove it in our faces. Not that he needed to, he was bigger and stronger than us in human form, and even bigger as a wolf.

I didn't dispute the need to go and see Fagua before Sky lost control and would need to be dragged out of the hotel suite. It wasn't a pretty sight at the best of times, and even worse when there were guests around. We needed to maintain an image, after all we owned the casino.

"I don't even know if your silver tongue is gonna help in this case. She looked ready to bolt earlier."

Sky lifted the mini bottle of booze in a toast. "Good luck."

ky

My brothers deem me as weak, Winter nearly went as far as to say I was an alcoholic or on my way fast to be one. Our uncle Kingsley was one. I don't ever remember seeing him sober. He always had a bottle, not a glass, in his hand, and never a full one.

Wolves who had an issue with shifting or who haven't found their mate, tended to drink. Sex wasn't good enough for them because the only women they could fuck were humans, and their holes were too small to accommodate our fat cocks. Frustrated to the point of madness was not an understatement. No, we needed mates. For some reason their holes were bigger and could satisfy us completely. Yet, Winter never had this issue. In some ways he was the perfect one out of us three.

He hardly lost his temper at anything, and part of me both envied and hated him for it at the same time. Husk had his cigars, and I drank to calm me down until the situation with Fagua was complete with her surrender.

I had visions of us going up to the hotel room, her seeing us and thinking, three hot studs as she stripped down ready to please us. I didn't think she would be chasing after the weasel who had broken the deal and fucking married her.

Bastard. What the hell was he thinking?

He was a two-timing shit. I'd known it from the moment I'd met him, but Husk said maybe we could use him to our benefit. I didn't want to question how he came to the conclusion a gambler would be a good person to trust. I was surprised that she still wore the bracelet. I'd half-expected him to pawn it. We gave it to him to help her escape her small town. Gamblers are worse than drug addicts. At least, an addict's always looking for their next fix, so all you need to do is tell them to do something and they wouldn't step outside the box because they wanted their fix. Gamblers are sneaky bastards. They'll do anything and con anyone out of money just so they can gamble some more. They don't care who they hurt, which is why I crossed the line with Keith. My temper got the best of me, and I beat the shit out of him, nearly leaving him for dead. The fucker threatened to take Fagua from us. Demanded triple the agreed to price. How he'd tell the world about us and how we paid him to bring her to him.

My brothers didn't need to know about that. I'd taken care of it by dumping his ass at the hospital. I waited around to ensure he was stable. Once I had it confirmed, then I left. And the chance Fagua would find out the truth would never happen. Even without that information, it was going to be tough convincing her to trust us in the first place.

Imposible.

If she found out this was all staged, then

she'd be running out of the door. There would be no keeping her. We needed her to be willing otherwise it would all fall to the shits.

For now, our focus would be on keeping her happy. I would need my wolf strength to do that. I would have to give up drinking to be a better brother and man. I couldn't go on like this, pretending being an alpha and wolf was enough to get me by, because it wasn't. I could end up destroying the family, and even worse end up destroying my life.

agua

I had never been through a crowd with such haste in all my life. Sure, I had seen people on TV and movies do this, but it was completely different in real life. People didn't move out of the way or hear me when I said, "excuse me". Despite my walking up and down the casino, weaving in and out of crowds, and checking everywhere for Keith, I couldn't find him. Panic swelled beneath my breastbone.

It reminded me of a tale or two I'd heard

about one of the dad's back home, who went to work one day on the fields and never came back. They never knew he had gone, because all his clothes still hung in the closet. But somewhere along the line, Giles' dad had decided to leave him. He was a coward. He didn't even bother to tell them goodbye. I remembered one time in sixth grade, Giles told us the story. We had to write a piece on something memorable in our lives, and Giles wrote that.

The day my dad left us.

I still got chills just thinking of his story, and how even now, it haunted me as I couldn't find Keith.

I could tell Jane, our teacher, wasn't happy about him wanting to read it out loud, but part of me was jealous. Giles had some experience, some trauma in his life. My piece was about the time dad had forgotten to turn off the stove, and the fire department run by my uncle had to go out to put out an actual fire. Our fire brigade spent most of their time helping cats get down from trees or building a new house. It had been the first time my uncle said in over fifteen years, they'd had to put out an actual fire. Even though Mahad used the fire extinguisher, by the time they got there, it hadn't been much of a fire.

In front of me appeared Sky. He had dark hair and matching eyes, but if someone had asked me to sketch him, I couldn't. It was as if he was there in the room with us all, but he wasn't really. It was weird. It had been Winter was alone in the room with me, apart from the big one, Husk, who seemed to enjoy laughing at my situation.

I hated him just from first impressions.

After asking reception, I even checked with the guy at the roulette wheel if he had seen my husband. Stupid, because Keith did say it was an underground game, but I was desperate, wondering if anything Keith had actually said was true.

No one had seen Keith since earlier this evening. I used the hotel's desks phone and called Keith's cell. It went straight to voicemail and my stomach clenched. The hotel clerk gave me a sad look and said hotel security hadn't seen him either.

My legs felt weak, like they couldn't

support me anymore, and I leaned against the desk for support. My head spun. Oh god, it was true. There was no other explanation. Still a tiny part of me hoped I was wrong. Keith hadn't gone and left me with three hot weirdos. No, I'd make that two hot weirdos and one good guy.

What if someone had kidnapped him?

I mean he'd said he'd won, and we were going to celebrate? Why even call and tell me if he was just going to disappear?

"Um..." I licked my lips. "Can you check and see if my husband was in a game tonight?"

The hotel clerk nodded, but there was a pinch to the edges of her blue eyes. She typed some stuff on the computer, but then shook her head. "I'm sorry Mr. Keith Strong never checked into a game after..." She squinted back at her computer, "six o'clock tonight."

"But he won, right?"

"Are you ok?" I felt a hand on my shoulder.

I nodded because I recognized his voice from the moment he'd stepped behind me. Then again, it was that damn scent. It'd been everywhere since I'd left town. I hadn't noticed before, but it was as if being here had awakened something different inside of me. A power I hadn't even noticed I possessed. I couldn't stay here any longer than necessary, and I hate picking up scents. I just looked weird, sniffing like a damn dog all the time.

I shook my head, "What have you done with him?"

Winter laughed and just annoyed me even more. I fought the urge to turn and walk away from this stranger who stirred up so much in me, I was having a hard time making sense of it all.

"Can we go to the room and talk about this?"

I was the one who laughed this time, "Not with your two weird boyfriends. No. I'll check out and leave. This is the twenty-first century. I have rights. You can't come to the room and tell me you want to talk. I'm not stupid. I know what you really want…" Despite my bravado, I was breathy and couldn't stop staring at his full, perfect lips. My whole body felt hot, and my face felt like it was on fire.

This time, he wasn't laughing as he drew closer to me and said, "You can't leave. Keith left you here to pay off the debt. You have to stay."

"What is this 365 days cut to 30 days? I'm a citizen and I have rights. Rights to do whatever I want, and I don't need to stay and you can't make me." Though at the mention of the erotic movie, my flush grew even hotter. I should have said Beauty and the Beast. No, wouldn't have worked either. Saw...now there was a crazy horror that kept the terror front and center where it needed to be.

"Stay with me," he growled as he looked me in the eyes.

"Okay," I replied, but that wasn't the word I wanted to say.

What in the actual fuck was going on?

Winter smirked, the bastard, and glanced around.

Fuck you.

I was going to make him let go of my arm and scream for the life of me, like a normal woman in distress.

"Don't make a sound." His bright, sapphire gaze locked on me again.

But I didn't scream. I couldn't. It was as if the desire was stuck inside me, and nothing could make me do what I really wanted to do, which was run out of here as fast as I could and never come back.

"Let's go." He placed his hand on my lower back, and I hated him for making me walk side-by-side like one of the Stepford Wives. What the hell was wrong with me?

"Smile," he cooed.

I felt the corners of my mouth pull upward in a tight smile. The type I put on if I took a photo. The type I would use if I was bored, but didn't want anyone to know. I was fucking scared. Who was this guy and why couldn't I control my body?

One of the security guards came up to him and said, "Mr. Crescent, is everything in order here?"

Was this some type of joke?

This hypnotist, or whatever he was, grabbed ahold of my arm. He towered over me by at least six inches, and security was being asked if he was okay. I mean what was I going to do to Mr. Crescent? What could I do? I tried to open my mouth to yell this guy who was controlling me, and I couldn't even do that.

I couldn't do anything against this man.

"It's fine, Henry. Everything is in order here. We're just going to the suite."

Henry nodded as his dark eyes scanned me from head-to-toe, and then it was as if the security was happy with Winter's response and strolled away like he was going to a fucking picnic.

He kept leading me forward, but not in the direction of my room. Was he going to take me wherever he'd taken my husband? My stomach clenched. We were away from the casino and away from prying eyes. At the hotel's elevator doors, I looked around. We were alone. The lobby was ghostly-quiet with not a soul in sight.

"Stay with me," he said the words once again.

Helplessly, I climbed into the elevator with him, and the doors shut with a hollow thud. It was then I knew he'd put some kind of spell on me. I felt as if I breathed for the first time since he'd said the word, and I turned my nerves into steel as I tried not to panic. My eyes were wide open like a goldfish. I was too scared to look at him. If he could control me so easily, then what would he do to me? He could say anything like jump off the roof, and I would be powerless to stop. I squeezed my eyes shut. A scream burned on the back of my throat, but I couldn't utter a single sound.

I didn't know what else he would say. Then again, I didn't want to know.

Husk

I stood in front of the elevator doors, waiting for Fagua to come out. She was too thin. We would break her, even if we claimed her one at a time. Yet, she was the woman from the dream. The one we'd been waiting for, but I knew before we did anything with her, we would have to fatten her up. That could take all of thirty days. Winter said we should tell her she has to stay with us long; otherwise she would leave, and we needed her to surrender to us.

I did something I rarely did. I smiled as the

doors opened and I waited for her. Sky was in no state to talk to anyone. His nerves were out of control, and he'd had one too many from the mini bar. I had to drag him up here because he was nearly out of it. With his weight and size, I didn't think those tiny liquor bottles could get him into such a state so quickly.

As the doors opened and we faced each other, I knew Winter had said something to her. Why do I always have to clean up after my brothers? He'd memorized her, and she could only do and say what he wanted. He'd used his powers on her, and it would make her even more suspicious and hate us more than she already did.

Winter avoided my stare as Fagua stood frozen in the elevator with the doors wide open.

He pointed to me and said, "Don't."

Which meant he probably blamed me for having to do things this way.

"Come in. Don't be shy," I continued to smile at her, and was when I realized that was probably why she shook like a leaf. We had a client meeting once and everything was going well until I'd smiled at the client's wife. Winter said, it was because when I smiled, I showed all my teeth and gums, and it wasn't an attractive sight, which was why I tended to avoid smiling like the plague.

"Drop it, Winter." I said, going back to my normal expression.

My brother pressed his fingers against her shoulder, and the glaze in her eyes vanished.

Instead of moving into our suite and being in awe like most of the women we'd ever brought up here, she shoved Winter back. He only moved a step away, and she dashed back into the elevator. Her fingers frantically pushed all the elevator buttons when one didn't work.

Sweat beaded across her brow as the elevator doors stayed open.

"You need a key to make the elevator work," I said with all the calmness and patience, to reassure her we weren't going to attack her.

"Okay," she quivered. She avoided looking at me and her gaze traced across the suite. "And I suppose neither one of you will give me a key?"

Winter and I shook our heads.

She straightened, stepping out of the

elevator and into our living quarters.

Our suite was the best in the casino. We'd had it refurbished to meet our every need, which included having our own space. We'd taken over the whole of the top floor, which our financial advisor said wasn't the best financial decision, but we didn't give a shit. No one had a top floor apartment apart from us, and we needed soundproof flooring for when Sky broke out and needed to go for a fly. We knew he would turn eventually. It had been just a matter of timing.

She moved hesitantly a little deeper into the open living room. Then faced me. "Where's Keith? What have you done with my husband?"

I looked past her to Winter who gave me a sour look. She clearly didn't believe Kevin had run off.

Winter used his powers, and he was probably angry at himself for doing it. Sometimes, it was needed, but whenever he was in human form, he hated it, which didn't make any sense. He couldn't use his powers after he shifted. That was our drawback, some wolves could talk when they shifted. Not us. We stayed in our true form whenever we shifted in and out.

"Fagua," I said as gently as I could and she stiffened. "Your husband lost his bet. Everything."

"No. That's not possible." She shook her head vehemently, her voice cracking. "H-he called me. Told me everything he planned had happened like he wanted."

I held my hand out to her. "Come."

Fagua stared at my palm as though it was a viper.

"I won't bite…unless you ask me to," I said.

Her blush made her dark eyes appear to glow. Fuck, she was beautiful, and if we got more meat on her skinny ass bones, she'd be mind-blowing gorgeous. No wonder shit-faced weasel had married her. Whatever rock he crawled under, he better stay there or I'd smash in his face.

Winter opened his mouth to speak, and I shot him *a don't you fucking dare* glare. He stepped back, giving Fagua space. Smart. Doubtful she wanted anything to do with him after he forced her to come here against her will.

"No." She crossed her arms over her chest. "Not until you take me to my husband."

"I can't do that."

"Then fuck you. I'm out of here." She spun on her heel, then looked at me over her shoulder. "Let me out now, or I won't stop screaming until either you both let me go or the police come."

Winter raked a hand through his white hair with his eyebrows raised as though silently asking if I wanted him to do his magic on her again.

"We can't take you to your husband because we don't know where he is either."

Slowly, Fagua turned around, looking from me to Winter and back again. "What do you mean?"

"If you haven't guessed, we own this hotel and casino." I shrugged a shoulder. "You are welcome to see for yourself about your husband on the surveillance cameras."

She placed a hand on her hip. "And how do I know whatever you show me is real, and you didn't fake it somehow?"

"We'll let you decide for yourself," Winter said, coming up on her right.

After a pause, she nodded. "All right. Show me."

Fagua

"This way," said Winter as he took the lead without looking back. "You can view the casino and hotel footage yourself."

Then again, what did he have to worry about? Wasn't like I could leave without their key. And we were on the top floor of a high-rise hotel, so climbing down or jumping was out of the question. Still, I was curious to see what the cameras might show and find out where they had taken Keith. I strolled through the apartment to the hallway despite my heart racing a mile a minute.

One room immediately to our right was open with flashing screens of so many things, I blinked, trying to focus on what I was seeing. "What is all this?"

"Live footage." He replied, before sitting in a black leather chair, and then he gestured for me to take the one next to him.

"Husk, you want a beer?" Winter asked.

"Yeah," he answered, pushing buttons on the control panel.

"Would you like anything, Fagua?" Winter looked expectantly at me, and then stood up to leave.

If I said the key out of here, I doubt he'd honor my request. "A glass of wine if you have any."

Husk snorted beside me. "If we don't, we'll have it delivered."

"There's cabernet sauvignon." Winter waited in the doorway for my answer.

"Perfect. Thanks."

Winter left and I turned back to the screens.

"What time did your husband call you from

the hotel room?" Husk asked, enlarging some shots and shrinking others.

"About twenty minutes before you three showed up at the door." And freaked me out. I crossed my legs, starting at the cameras and willing them to show my husband.

Husk flipped some switches and pointed to one of the screens. "That's him, right?"

I squinted because it looked like Keith from the back, but there was a blond on his arm. "No, that's not him—"

But then he turned toward the camera with a smile, the blond giggled, and my heart froze. Keith kissed the woman on the mouth and handed her his drink before walking to the casino's phones. He picked up the handset, and Husk did something to turn up the volume. Keith's voice came through the speakers.

I placed a trembling hand over my mouth, shaking my head.

After Keith hung up, the woman with her purse looking like a gold suitcase joined him. Together they strolled out of the casino. Without asking, Husk moved to another camera angle, enlarging it to show Keith climbing into a convertible with the woman and driving down the road.

"No." I pulled my hand away from my face. "This has to be a mistake. Keith is married to me. He wouldn't do this. He wouldn't leave me for some other woman he just met." But wasn't that what he'd done with me? Took me up on my request to come to Vegas then proposed on the way. Oh god, were we even really married or was it some big con he set up? Emotions slammed into me, and I wasn't sure if I was going to cry or scream.

Of course, we hadn't consummated the marriage and it could be annulled.

What was the whole point?

I didn't get why he took me and helped me leave town. It was as if I'd been struck by a bolt of lightning as the answer to my question, slowly, but surely, was being answered.

"Fagua," Husk said my name in such a soft, caring tone I jumped up out of the chair.

"You're wrong. Th-this is a trick. You planned to bring me here and show this, and you doctored the footage to make me believe something isn't true." Tears stung my eyes. I blinked them back, clutching my fists. The first man to ever pay attention to me was a fake, and he used me to pay a hotel bill. This was why he was quick to get rid of me once we arrived. He probably figured it would be easier to hitchhike as a couple than alone. And the car. The one he'd entered with her, it must have been hers. Like me, Keith had probably conned her, too.

"No, I'm afraid nothing's been altered or changed in any way." Husk leaned back. "If you don't believe me, you can talk to our security or anyone in the casino or hotel staff. Or you can ask the police to pull up traffic light footage, and it will show you exactly what you've seen here."

I sank back into the leather chair. "Fucking bastard cheated on me, and we haven't even picked out stupid rings yet."

Winter returned with a bottle of beer for Husk and himself, then handed me a glass of ruby-red wine. I accepted the drink from him and gulped it down, as if it were a glass of water, because as soon as it was empty, I would be handing it to him for a refill. In the space of less than a week, I'd fallen in love, escaped from the one place I knew as home, and had lived all my life, to getting married, to being sold to wolves. I needed something stiffer next time. I intended to get well and truly drunk.

"Slow down there," Winter said, but I guess he didn't use his compulsion on me, because I didn't listen.

"God, I can't believe this is happening. First, I thought I'd be stuck in my silly, little town forever. Then I got a husband and jilted all in less than a week." I seethed.

"Who the hell was the woman he was with? Get her license plate and track her down." Did she even know Keith was married or did she just not care?

The phone rang, and Winter stepped out into the hallway to answer.

Somehow, I believed Husk and Winter about Keith. A huge part of me didn't want to, but I couldn't even tell them I'd had evidence of Keith being a con man before, and I ignored it. Like how Ray Hope, the owner of our local motel and someone I'd known my whole life had said Keith had an outstanding bill. I'd paid his hotel bill because he'd said he'd forgotten. Now I was paying the price with my heart. All his fancy talk and promises were like fool's gold, and I'd fallen for it.

Husk drank his beer and watched me with hooded eyes. "You're going to be okay."

"Am I?" I shuddered, the warmth of the alcohol flushing my skin.

Winter poked his white head into the room. "We got a lead. Sylvia Mullins just called the cops saying she was robbed by one of our guests."

"The woman in Keith's car?" I asked, already knowing in my gut it was true.

"Yeah." Winter gave me a soft smile and made me feel a little calmer. "Do you want to speak with her?"

I nodded despite the taste of bile rising into the back of my throat. Slowly, I pushed up from the chair. My legs felt numb as I crossed the distance between us. I took his phone, and he stepped back, giving my privacy.

"Hello? Mrs. Mulligans?"

"Who is this?" a female voice said over the line. "Is this the casino? I demand a refund on my winnings. Keith said he worked for you and he stole everything."

"No, I'm—" I couldn't say I was Keith's wife.

Not after what he'd done to me. The betrayal felt like an icy knife continually stabbing me in the chest. "I'm afraid he robbed me, too." Of my peace-of-mind, of my heart, of my future with him.

"Oh." She paused. "He told me we were going to get married, and he just needed to stop off at my house to get ready. When I came out, he was gone. He took my casino chips, my money, even my freaking car."

I squeezed my eyes shut, tears threatening to spill. I was going to need not another drink, but the whole damn bottle after this. "I'm so sorry. H-He'll pay for what he's done to you and me and however many victims he has in his past." I opened my eyes and handed Winter back his phone.

Winter strolled out of the room, his voice was soothing as he spoke with the woman.

For a long time, I stared at the screens showing everything from people jumping up and down from winning on the slots to people storming out because they'd lost.

"Here." Husk was beside me with an opened beer in his hand.

I hadn't even noticed he left.

"Not that I'm condoning alcohol to take away your troubles, but in this case, I think it calls for it."

I took a moment, realizing the man, the wolf I was so scared of, may have a gentle side.

"Thanks." I nodded, and he opened the beer for me before handing it over. This time, I didn't guzzle it down, but held onto it like it was a lifeline.

Winter returned with his blue eyes pinched in the corners. I guess he felt bad about me and Sylvia getting taken in by a con artist.

"Never thought I'd come to Vegas," I lifted my beer in a mock toast. "Yet here I am with my world turned upside down."

Husk gave Winter a look set my stomach churning.

"What?" I sipped my beer. "Tell me or I'll probably imagine much worse."

Winter opened his mouth, but then shook his head. "You tell her. I don't want her to think I'm making her believe anything."

"Someone better tell me." Though part of me didn't want to know. The part which had been asleep back home while I had gone through my day on autopilot.

Involuntarily, I grabbed at the crystal necklace Keith had given me when I'd first met him.

"You have to stay with us for thirty days."

He commanded as if he owned me or something, I stuttered as I asked, "What are you talking about?"

He repeated, "Thirty days."

Oh shit, the fucking poker game. The one Keith lost, and traded me in for. I really had no option, I had nowhere to go and realistically nowhere to stay.

Husk

I didn't move as she stared at me like I was the craziest person she'd ever seen. If she only knew half the things I'd done in my life, she wouldn't be far off.

"Are you saying my husband sold me to—to the three of you?" She shook her head as though she couldn't believe what I'd said.

"Yes. And you will stay here with us for the next thirty days."

Finishing her beer, she stood and walked out of the video room while I watched her intensely, waiting for her to break out as she had done before or show some kind of rage. I could only assume the reason she was so calm was from the two glasses of wine, and now her beer. I followed her as if she'd memorized how to get here and ended up back at the lobby. I signaled for her to follow me to the living room.

She stopped as she stared at the view, the glass wall facing the swimming pool. I could tell she wanted to go out for some fresh air. So I opened the door for her. With the click of a button, it slid open. It used to be automatic, but then Sky would run past it and nearly drown in the damn pool, one too many times. He roamed around this place like a caged wolf, especially, because he didn't know how to swim. Crazy, he could fly, but couldn't swim.

"The view from here's amazing. I've never seen something so beautiful."

I shook my head as the once frightened woman who had stepped into the penthouse, turned with bright eyes as she looked over at me.

The strange part was until she mentioned it, I'd never thought of the view as beautiful. I looked out, not thinking about anything, but trying to see the same beauty which she had described a few seconds ago. As the sun set, the Vegas strips lights all came alive at the same time. Every building ranging from gold, to white, to blue, it was as if the bouncing of the lights from each building made it seem as if the buildings were dancing to music built from the buzz of the city.

I stood beside her, "I'm sorry about Keith."

Keith had married her without our approval, and then demanded more money for bringing her to us. I hated him, and I just hoped to never see him again or I would lose control.

"I don't even have a ring to hock." She wiped at the corner of her eye.

"No?"

I wanted confirmation. He didn't not have a ring, but there was something else missing to confirm the marriage to him was real.

Had she fucked him?

She leaned against the railing, looking out across the city with the twinkling lights below us. "I pay my debts even if they're someone else's. I have nowhere to go. I don't even know if I'll be allowed back home, or even if I want to go back there…" Her shoulders hunched slightly. "Should've known never to trust a stranger."

"We're strangers, Fagua." I faced her, leaning my side against the balcony's railing. "And I trust you."

"Maybe you shouldn't." Her dark gaze challenged me.

A smile tugged at the corners of my mouth, and I fought the urge to draw her into my arms and kiss her until she clung to me and moaned my name. "I can handle anything you dish out."

Then, she looked back out on the city. "Could be worse, I guess. At least I'm in a hotel casino's penthouse and not chained up in a basement."

"That's for next week," I teased, and she laughed.

She was ours, and I was never going to let her go. Never going to stop making her happy and spending the rest of my life making up the fact we paid to have her brought to us.

I held out my hand. "How about I give you a tour of everything, then I'll let you get settled."

For an instant, I thought she'd balk and demand to be freed to go home. Instead, she turned to me and lifted her head, taking my hand. I drew her over to the pool's bar and pushed the remote and opened the big screen dropped down.

"We even have our own outdoor cinema."

"Oh my God!" She screamed out as she drew near to the hot tub, her hand pulling from mine. "And a jacuzzi too? Holy cow!"

I was about to tell her to be careful, she could slip on the tiles, and knowing Winter he would probably blame me for the accident and claim I scared her somehow.

"I could sit in this all day and just watch the view. I wouldn't watch TV. I mean what's the point of being out here if all you're going to do is watch the big screen?"

She waited for an answer, but I didn't give her one, because part of me knew she had a valid point and the other part of me hated her for making it. We were privileged, and we did nothing to enjoy it. I had to get myself under control, so I did what I always did in these types of circumstances, I lit up a cigar and as the fumes started to move down my throat and calm my nervous system. Giving her space, I laid down on one of the lounge chairs while she looked around outside.

Closing my eyes, I wanted to tell her not to worry about Keith, about what an asshole he was for leaving her. But then I would be tempted to tell her the truth...how we paid him to bring her here. How no rival wolf could get within a mile of her dad's little town. But then I'd probably blow any chance with her to heal us.

"Are you sleeping?" she asked as she stepped up to me and prodded me as if I was dead.

"No, just reflecting," I barked back. I expected her to be scared, but she surprised me by sniggering as she carried on taking in the view as she walked up to the hot tub.

She sank into the sun chair next to me, and it was as if she was doing it to lose her thoughts.

I spoke to break the silence, I wanted to know what was on her mind.

"Are you okay being here for thirty days?"

I got right to the point.

"Yes." She closed her eyes and looked so much like a goddamn angel my heart squeezed.

The patio door slid open, and Winter came

out and joined us. Might as well let him in on our conversation.

"Winter told you the time you would be staying here?"

"Yes."

He crept behind me and shook his head, which meant he hadn't told her. I wondered what he had told her, but then I could tell she was either exhausted from today, or she just wanted to be left alone.

I motioned to Winter and stood. We'd go back inside and talk, leaving her to rest. He started heading back.

As I started to join Winter, she blurted, "You're a wolf aren't you?'"

I stood frozen, unable to look at her.

I kept on walking, she knew the answer to her own question and as we arrived safely back into the penthouse I said to Winter.

"She knows."

He didn't say a word. Instead he beckoned for me to follow him, and I did just as I stumped out my cigar and went to Sky's room.

agua

Werewolves.

Husk and Winter were both gorgeous and made my body heat in ways I hadn't even imagined when Keith and I had fooled around. Actually, no one had ever made me feel this way. My entire life was like I balanced on a high wire, both terrified I would fall to my death and thrilled about making it all the way across.

I wanted to get out of here from the moment

I arrived. I knew the secrets of our town, the real reason why Pa settled in the smallest and quietest town in the middle of the woods. Yes, the woods. It was because we were a town of wolves, and I had no mate. I hadn't been claimed by one of the two brutes of the town.

I wanted to leave from the moment I'd gotten here, but I knew I would have to do it with their permission. All because my human husband had sold me to them for thirty freaking days. Can't believe I trusted the jerk. Should've known he was a manipulating con man.

And what about these three werewolves? They would have to let me go, and the one I thought I felt a bond with, wasn't the case at all. Winter had powers, something I never knew existed among full-blooded werewolves.

Back home, I used to dream of a werewolf sweeping me off my feet and carrying me to some far off-place. Once when I had mentioned it to Ma, she forbade me from saying anything ever again on the topic. I pretended not to know other werewolves outside our town existed, but my senses had been on fire since I'd met these three, it had been pretty hard to ignore them.

I sat by the hot tub, and hoped they would forget about me, because I wouldn't let them claim me. I'd reject them from the moment they tried. Besides, once they realized I wasn't interested then they would have to let me go. They could have any woman they wanted. Well, Winter could. The other two would have difficulty, because as friendly as Husk had been a few seconds ago, I couldn't get over the way he'd made me feel at first.

I smelled their ages. They weren't young wolves, apart from the creepy one. Sky, I think they said was his name. The one hardly spoke.

"Dinner's ready," a voice said behind me.

I jumped up and he said, "Sorry, didn't mean to scare you. You've been here for over five hours."

"Really?"

I'd been here longer than I thought. It was the view, so breathtaking I'd forgotten how long I'd been here. It had changed from day to night until I watched the lights illuminate the city.

"Anyway, we thought seeing as you like

being outdoors so much, you would want to eat here," Winter pointed at the table which was candlelit. His brothers were sat opposite the outdoor kitchen, which was bigger than the one we had in the diner.

How nice it must be to be rich?

His brothers sat waiting to be served by the chef who was furiously cooking and barbecuing at the same time.

As I stepped down, I realized I'd been harsh. Husk got up and helped the Chef on the grill. They barbecued fillet mignons, and my mouth watered.

Husk turned to face me and said, "Do you want to freshen up before dinner?"

I lifted my arm and sniffed my armpit, a natural reaction I did back home.

"Why do I smell?"

I forgot I was in the company of wolves, for a minute as they burst out laughing. The Chef had no idea what was going on as he smiled at me, and then turned back to the cooker in confusion.

"No, sit down," Husk commanded.

I bristled, but I was also starving and refused the idea of denying myself food merely to prove a point. I hated the alpha wolf bullshit. It was stupid. Besides, fainting from lack of food wasn't smart while I was a prisoner in this pretty palace with three strangers...three werewolves who made me want to stay and learn more about them. Where they were from and how they had become so rich and to own a place like this?

"We've got it from here. You can leave now," Husk turned off the cooker and gave a look that would have sent many wolves back home whimpering into a submissive pose.

The Chef made a quick exit, but he mumbled something, but I could tell he was probably wondering what was going on, then his exit told me my first impression had been right.

Winter pulled a chair out for me, bowing his head slightly.

"Thanks," I said as I sat.

It made me feel a little relaxed, but not enough to let my guard down and talk all night to them. We had nothing to talk about. I was nothing like them, and I think as alpha as they were, and wanted to be, when I told them I knew their other form, they'd appeared shocked. I did have some abilities like height-ened sense of smell, for example.

The Chef returned with a huge dish from inside the penthouse. Steam rolled from the food, and he set it on the table in front of us. This was when it hit me, they weren't treating me like a prisoner, but rather a guest.

What had Keith done for me?

Nothing but used me. They were trying to be hospitable.

"Right, that's all from me guys and lady," the Chef bowed his head and returned a second later with plates and utensils for us.

A perfect blend of spiciness, hot cheese, and chicken made me want to crawl across the table and dive inside everything.

"How about some more light?" Winter stood and lit a few torch-like stands around us, giving a glow like candlelight and softening the night around us. It was almost like we were in our own little world.

Husk put down every assortment of meat. It seemed as if he'd prepared steak, ribs, chicken and sausages. I was tempted to ask if other people were joining us. The table was full of meat, salad, pasta and different types of bread under the sun. This was just dinner. I hated to think what they had for breakfast and lunch? Seriously, all the food here could feed a dozen people easily, but they were not people I had to remind myself they were wolves. I should be used to seeing rows of food being divulged in such a short time.

"You've done a good job, Ralph," Husk said as he admired the table. It was weird to see him friendly. On first impressions, he clearly was the alpha, and I expected him to be the type couldn't be nice to anyone, yet he seemed to have no problem with the Chef.

"Any time, you're easily pleased."

Winter laughed. "Husk is, he eats everything and anything. He has more than a healthy appetite!."

Husk winked at him, as a roar of laughter left their mouths. There was too much testosterone for me to deal with, it was as if I was the only delicate flower among these brutes.

Sky tried to get up, no doubt to walk Chef out, but he refused, and Sky promptly sat down as if he was happy about the idea of not having to stand. This was when I noticed his eyes were slightly slanted, as if had either just awakened, or was extremely tired. Then, all of a sudden they all started grabbing the meat and shoving it in their mouths. I didn't even know if they were chewing their food. It felt as if they were swallowing it as they grabbed it with their hands, as if the cutlery and plates on the table were for decoration, much like the candles. The meat never hit their plates. It went straight from the serving dish, head up and down their throats. Even Pa and the rest of the men in my family were civilized when we all sat down together. Not these three. The little appetite I'd had earlier had flown off the rooftop as they made animal noises and devoured the meat. I wondered if they'd left the chicken, salad, and spaghetti for me. Neither one of them touched those three items on the table. It was as if they'd satisfied their hunger at once as they stopped and all three looked at me. The same way they did when they'd come into the hotel room.

"Are you not going to eat?" Husk commanded. But it didn't feel like a question, it was more of a demand.

I sighed, trying to hide my hunger, but

wanting to put them in place. "Not without saying grace first."

It was a lie, and I could feel it embarrassed them as I said it, which is what I wanted to do. I couldn't remember the last time I'd said grace before eating. When Grandma was alive, we did it all the time as a kid, but my parents were half in and half out when it came to Christianity. Ma was in, and Pa was out.

"Of course," Winter said. "Where are our manners?"

Husk grunted. "We're wolves, not men. We don't possess them."

"Don't I know it," I intended to say quietly, but seeing as Husk rocked my boat, I said it directly to him.

"Can everyone calm down," Sky said "We'll say grace, and we did forget our manners. We're not used to company when we eat, and Husk tends to eat most of the food, because he eats the quickest. So, Winter and I follow, before it's all gone."

My stare met Husk's as he waited for me to challenge him. I said nothing, but bowed my head ready to say grace. Sky felt as if he had to explain their behavior to me. Maybe he wasn't as creepy as I thought he was, because he did tend to have some manners.

I waited a few seconds, not looking at them, I could tell they were copying me, as I no longer heard the sound of the meat going down their throats. Instead my ears were met only by the sounds of the gentle breeze.

"Dear Lord, Thank you for my health and my family. Thank you for allowing me to have some food, left on the table primarily the chicken and salad. I want to ask you Lord, please keep me safe, from any harm."

I stopped to open my eyes, curious to see if they were actually praying; their heads were bowed down, but they shifted uncomfortably in their seats. Sky and Winter did, but Husk just kept his head bowed down like a statue. I was surprised by their reactions.

"Thank you, Lord, for always protecting me and keeping me safe from these animals. Amen."

I shouldn't have used the Lord like that. I couldn't stay here with three werewolves who had bought me. I wouldn't be their slave or anything else they wanted. I just had to figure out what to do next, how to get out of this situation.

"Fuck this." Husk jumped up as if his seat were on fire. "We're not in church, and I won't be preached to by a woman who can't be courteous as a guest with us going out of our way to please her." He grabbed a bottle of red wine with the opener, setting both down on the table. He took my plate, filled it with the chicken, spaghetti and salad.

Then he barked, "Come with me!"

"Don't. She can sit out here with us," Winter protested.

Husk didn't even say a word to him, but just gave him a deadly stare.

I followed Husk across the rooftop. We entered he white kitchen through different entrance, then we'd used when I'd first came to the suite. I took in the brand new appliances, which shone black with the marble floor and matching workspace. I bet they've never even cooked in here.

I picked up the pace to catch up with him as he walked through the white hallway. There were photos up on the wall and I wanted to take a closer peek except he walked so fast I found myself jogging behind him.

At a wooden door, he kicked it open all the way. Everything looked the damn same. I couldn't leave, even if I wanted to, because I would get lost, it was a white maze.

Husk dropped the plate, wine and opener on the table and said, "Eat here, alone, and while you're at it, you can think about your husband. You know, the one who gave you to us. Who ran out on you the second he could."

I assumed this was my room, as I spotted a rustic suitcase with what looked to be a door to a bedroom. The food still steamed, and I licked my lips, dying to eat all of it from the moment the Chef had placed it on the table. Instead, I said, "You forgot to bring cutlery."

Husk shook his head and said, "No, you forgot to pick it up!"

He slammed the door and left, with no intention of bringing the cutlery. I could go back there, but I had no idea how we got to the room in the first place. Besides I was too scared to leave. I headed to what I assumed was the en-suite. Why the heck did all the doors have to be white?

"Holy cow," I screamed out as I walked into the closet, which was clearly not the bathroom, and proceeded to open every white door, until I found what I needed. I'd wash my hands and eat. At least I didn't have to eat with those animals, even if I had to eat with my hands. Husk thought he could break me by locking me in a huge en-suite? I stifled a laugh. He and the others had no idea. I'd gone twenty-five years locked in a small, backward werewolf town. My Ma and Pa didn't allow me to go anywhere except school, church, and the diner once I was old enough to work. I even still lived at home because I wasn't allowed to leave until I was married. A woman only left her parents whenever she married. I had tried for years to leave town and see the world. And it was only until I met Keith that I was able to leave. Every time before then, I'd lost interest and the desire to race back home was over-whelming. I made my way back to the room with the plate Husk had dumped onto the table.

How the hell was I supposed to eat spaghetti with my hands?

I was about to find out!

CHAPTER 9

*S*ky

Usk needed to control his fucking temper. He'd lost it with her, and I think at this rate, she'd be staying one night, not thirty. Winter and I were silent as we waited for him to come back. I didn't even feel like eating any more, or even having a drink. The thirst I had for food, and to claim her, were doused when Husk completely lost his cool.

As though on cue, Husk stomped to the

table and plopped down, grabbing his beer and taking a long drawl.

"What the fuck man, not cool. Not cool at all." I pushed my plate away. My gaze darted to it for a second. I thought it was stupid bringing them out in the first place. We never ate from them.

He waved his hands up in the air, and at times I used to wonder if he really was a wolf, or a lion in disguise. He always seemed to roar whenever he did that.

"She insulted us by pretending she was hell bent on praying. Implying we were animals that had no manners!"

Winter arched his eyebrow, "Well, we are wolves.

Husk waved his finger in the air. "Not in this form. We're human, just like her."

My eyes darted to Winter, who merely shrugged and sat down. When Husk was in one of his fuck it, I'm fucking right moods, we knew better than to prove him wrong. Besides, I was exhausted. It'd been one long day. I hadn't told my brothers about Keith, and when she was praying, I was a little freaked out. It was as if she had some kind of six-sense and she was worried we would hurt her. Like I had done with Keith. Winter was the easy-going among the three of us. Guess it was because he could make anyone do pretty much anything with his voice. We used to kid him his real mother must have been a siren.

"Do you think she has powers? Other than one of healing?" I asked, scratching my head, ignoring Husk's rants. Part of me hoped they hadn't heard me, but I had to get the suspicion off my chest.

"Fuck! What have you done?" Winter asked as though he realized there was a good reason for my question. He'd read me better than I would have thought, and I couldn't stop myself from cringing.

Husk didn't say a word, which meant he was all ranted out, but then as he grabbed another steak, I realized he was just hungry, and this was the real reason for his outburst. He didn't mind being interrupted with sleep, work or anything else, but when it came to feeding, he went crazy.

I took a deep breath, "Now don't go all crazy shit on me. But she had a point in her prayer. About worrying about us hurting her.

We haven't threatened her, so then I'm thinking if she's psychic or something, because I did do something to Keith."

Husk wiped his mouth and said, "Good, I hope you took pictures so we can show it to her, and that'll keep her mouth shut."

Winter shook his head, I ignored his comment and carried on.

"So, I told him his job was done. He could go, his debt was wiped free, and then he said something about he'd been entertaining her on their car trip up here, and we needed to compensate him for his efforts."

Husk started laughing, which meant he was nearly full. "Get to the point. You've already told us, he wanted more money."

"I asked how much he wanted and he said a cool million. I said, "cool", he said yeah, we take from the wheel each month. He was asking for pennies, and we could give it to him in a heartbeat."

"Shit. He really was a weasel, but we had no choice, we had to use him. If we went to Small-Heath, they would have killed us before we'd even reached the town. Wolves get killed.

Humans get to stay, or they stop over before leaving," Winter said.

Husk cut into his steak, and before putting a piece into his mouth said, "I want to know what happened to Keith."

I thought of how best to continue my story as I nibbled on the last remains of the sausage.

"Well, I told him he's lucky we didn't kill him, and he said go on then."

"Wrong words to say to a wolf," Husk said between chews.

"Fucking right. I roughed him up a bit. A bit more than I should have..."

I was stalling.

"And?" Husk asked as he clearly lost his patience.

"I took him to the hospital, made sure he was stable, and then left."

"At least you did one decent thing," Winter sighed as he got up and stepped away.

"I thought I was the one with the temper."

"You are," Winter and I said in unison to Husk.

"At least you didn't kill him." Winter sat back down and leaned back in his chair.

"Good, at least he's not here. Did you take

him to the hospital, and say you was the one to beat the crap out of him. Please Sky, just don't bother bullshitting. You couldn't have given him a slap or two and then taken him to the hospital to make sure he was stable," Husk wiped his mouth and threw down his napkin on his empty plate. "You should have just killed him, it would have been easier."

Husk stood while Winter and I waited for him to leave. He didn't wait for a response. We didn't have to say what was on our mind. We were not brought up that way, and we never killed unless we were defending ourselves and a little weasel like him couldn't do any harm to our family, no matter how hard he threatened.

Something troubled Husk, and I suspected it had everything to do with our mate. She'd gotten to him. He wanted to kill Keith, not because he wanted money from us, but simply because Fagua was his wife.

Fagua

I loved my room, don't get me wrong. I've never had anything as nice as this. From the king sized bed with bed posts, to the silk sheets, and the en-suite, which had a separate bath and shower. The bathroom alone was at least twice as big as my room back home.

Four long days had passed and I hadn't seen the brothers. Not that I wanted to see them. Winter, I wouldn't mind seeing. Sky was a possibility, but by no means did I ever want to see Husk again. I've marked a line on the wall to mark how long I've been here, like a prisoner. The same way they did in the movies. I did it partly so I would know how long I've been here and the other part was just to wind up Husk. Anything to get under his tail. The idea of it all made me laugh, knowing I'd rocked his boat so hard he didn't want me to sit at the table with him and eat.

Typical alpha.

They walked around as if they owned everyone and everything around them. It was as if they thought the world belonged to him. This was the life I was trying to get away from, and somehow I'd landed right into the middle of it.

I kicked at the couch out of frustration.

Damnit!

Pain shot up the ball of my foot.

There was a knock on the door. I hopped on one foot and glanced at the crystal antique clock on the wall. It wasn't breakfast, lunch, or dinner time. Those were the only times I put on a shirt and pants, so no one knew I'd been in my pj's all day. I had nowhere to go, and it seemed weird being in a bedroom and not being in my pj's. Especially, seeing as for the last four days, I'd done nothing but stay here.

Luckily, they had Netflix and Prime, so at least TV wasn't too boring. I had enough series and Netflix to binge, and I'd been eating too much. Every meal consisted of at least two or three options. Maybe this was their plan, to keep me here for thirty days and fatten me up and turn me into a zombie. If it was the plan, then it was working. There was nothing to do. I couldn't even access the pool or hot tub from this room. Damn, I really had wanted to try out both.

"May I come in?" Winter asked as he knocked harder against the door, and my heart skipped a beat.

"One minute."

I made a quick dive to the bathroom, my pants and shirt for the day hung in there. Whenever there was a knock on the door at one of the meal times, then I would dash in here. Change, smile and thank him. Until now, I had resisted the urge to ask him questions or plead to be released. But even my stubbornness was chipping away from being bored out of my mind and without human contact aside from him dropping off three meals a day,

I did a quick check of my hair in the mirror. Well, it was as good as I could get my straight, dark hair without any utensils other than a brush or hair product. All they had in this bathroom was soap, shampoo and conditioner. Seeing how there was nothing else I could do, not even dab on lipstick or mascara, I moved swiftly to the door and opened it.

"Hi," Winter said, standing as if he were nervous. He wore a blue suit which highlighted his sapphire eyes and white hair. He looked like a modern-day Viking with a haircut and always clean-shaven, while Husk acted like a damn Berserker whenever someone ticked him off.

"Come in," I stepped aside and waved an arm out. "After all, it's your suite."

"Yes, and we want you to feel comfortable." He entered and left the door open behind him. "You don't have to lock yourself in here. That wasn't the plan."

"What was the plan then? Lock me in here for thirty days and hope we'll all be mates and live happily ever after?" I laughed. Then the idea of what I'd said knocked me over because Winter didn't even flinch. Me? Be mates with all three of them? No, this was crazy. Maybe they hoped one of them would resonate with me. "You've got to be kidding me. That's not how this thing works. We need to feel a connection, and the only connection I've had with you guys is Husk telling me to eat in my room alone. Sky acts as if I'm a leper and you…"

He crossed his arms and nodded for me to go on.

"You tricked me into getting into the elevator with you. Put some spell on me to make me do what you wanted."

"You've been living among wolves for so long, but you're not one. I just didn't. Well, we didn't think you would know one wolf from the next." He offered me a smile. "We've never met someone like you before."

I shrugged, "I've never met anyone like any of you before, and I didn't mean what I said about you guys being animals."

I avoided meeting his stare.

"Yes, you did. You meant every word of it."

I chuckled. "I suppose I did."

An uncomfortable silence grew between us, and I didn't know what to say.

"I think you need to get to know us better.

Individually. If you like we can spend this afternoon by the pool."

Was he serious? I held my breath because maybe this was a dream brought on by boredom of staying here alone for four freaking days.

"Do you think we could start again?"

I slumped onto the couch as I weighed up the options. I could go back home. The place where everyone would laugh at me after the humiliation of not only returning married with no husband, but the way I left. I didn't even have the courage to tell them face-to-face. Just a note I left by my bedside. They'd want to know what happened to Keith. It'd only been a week, yet he'd married me and left me the next day.

No, I couldn't do that. The idea of going back there was too humiliating, but then what did twenty-six days mean here? I could put up a front, and then it would drag out, and I'd still end up going back home anyway with my worn-out suitcase and broken heart. Well, it wasn't as broken as I thought it would be when I had been told Keith had sold me. I was angry more than anything because it meant I would be stuck here. Honestly, I hadn't planned on marrying him. It just kinda happened. It had been a miracle when Keith and I had crossed the town's border. I hadn't wanted to go straight back. I kept waiting for the feeling I always had when I got this far. The overwhelming nausea or desire to run as fast as I could back home, but it never came, even when we crossed into Vegas. So when Keith asked me to marry him, I didn't even think it through, believing we had come together by fate. What a joke. Especially finding out he's done it to someone else. Taken her money and lied to her. I didn't even understand why he was even on my mind. He should be the last person I thought about!

I was on my own. I had no choice but to come up with an escape plan, even if the three werewolves weren't treating me like a prisoner. If anything, I was the one was acting like it.

The pros and cons were too much, and they hurt my head. I had waitressing skills. I could get a job. I didn't have to go back home. I was selling myself short.

"I'll leave you to think about it." Winter moved towards the door, ready to leave.

He wanted me to have fun and the only thing I could think about was escaping.

I shrugged, "Fine. We can have lunch together."

"Good." His smile was electric. "I was hoping you would say that. I'll meet you by the tub in an hour."

Really? It was time already?

"No. I don't know how to get there from here, I haven't left this area since I got here, and this place is like a white maze."

"I'll come and pick you up in an hour." He opened the door and stepped out into the hallway.

"But, I don't have a swimsuit." I had been in such a hurry to leave town with Keith I had forgotten to bring one.

"Everything you need has been ordered for you and will be delivered shortly," Winter said. "I'll pick you up in an hour."

True to Winter's word, about ten minutes after he left, a knock sounded on the door. Three women showed up with smiles, each carrying several bags overflowing with items.

"Would you like us to hang these up for you?" one of the women asked.

"No, that's okay, I can do it." It felt weird to have them bringing me clothes at all. "Let me get you all a tip." I rushed to my purse.

"That's okay, we've already been more than compensated," another woman said. "More clothes and shoes will be sent up later."

"Thanks." Just how many things had Winter ordered for me?

After the women left, I started pulling things out of one of the bags.

The first was a beaded black cocktail dress for evening wear, followed by sportswear, casual wear and even three bikinis and two swimsuits. Everything was in my size. I checked them all. They were all size six, and everything still had the tags on it, even the underwear. I could be wearing silky and lacey underwear instead of my tired cotton knickers.

I felt excited like a kid in a candy store as I threw them on the bed trying to think of which one to try on first.

I had a shower because it was such a big deal trying on so many new clothes. They all looked and smelled expensive, not the type of clothes I would buy from the local store.

Hell no! Some of them had designer labels such as Gucci and LV. This was every woman's dream.

Then I opened the other bag to see purses, jewelry like I'd never possessed in my life. A box, which had rings, necklaces and earrings. Expensive-looking with real diamonds and rose-gold. Everything in here felt unreal, as if they couldn't be mine. I picked up the earrings and without hesitation tried them on, then everything in the jewelry box. I assumed if I tried them all on, then they couldn't return them. I wanted them all for marrying a jerk and for having to live with these three wolves for twenty-six more days.

I felt silly, they'd fed me, given me a nice room, and I acted as if they were animals. I sighed as I thought about the way I'd treated them, when really Keith was the real jerk in this story. He'd lied and told me he had a big win. He could have told me the truth so we could run away together, but he didn't. He was too busy conning the next woman. My judgment had been clouded by wanting to leave the town I'd known all my life. The people I'd grown up with, who'd never treated me badly, and I'd thrown it away from some stranger who promised me the world and gave me nothing in return.

My head hurt. Too many things running through my mind and I had all of ten minutes to get ready. They were rich. The kind of people who could get anything they wanted by the snap of their fingers. I should stop worrying and just enjoy it.

I'd been watching the lives of the rich and famous for the last few days, and now I was living it for the month. I should embrace it, instead of rejecting it.

W inter

I was just about to knock when Fagua swung the door wide open. Her breasts hung slightly over her bikini. She must have put on a little weight in the time she'd been here. Husk was obsessed with her figure, then again, he was obsessed about everything about her.

"She's too skinny, rude, selfish, and intolerable. There's no way she's our mate."

Which meant that she must be our mate, and he knew it. This situation was new for all of us, not just him. Sky was coping with shifting, I was holding everyone together, especially with Husk's temper. Now, it was time for us to bond as a unit to complete our family and that meant Fagua was part of the equation.

"Ready?" She perked up.

"Sure. I didn't think you wanted to get in the hot tub yet."

She laughed. "I've been stuck in this room for four days. I can't think of anything better than being out in the fresh air."

Her positive attitude awed and surprised me.

She closed the door and followed me. Several times she bumped into me and mumbled an apology. When we finally reached the door to go outside, I held it open for her. She grinned, appearing to be relieved to be finally going out.

"I'll show you how to get out, so you can go by yourself anytime you wish. In case we're not around and you want to leave."

"Leave?" She hesitated. "Does this mean I can leave the suite?"

"Yes. But you must come back. You understand right? We don't want you to feel as if you have to stay in. We want you to have freedom, not like when you were in SmallHeath."

She opened her mouth like she was about to ask me how I knew, but I wanted us to get to the tub. We could talk then. No doubt she would have a lot of questions, and I was more than willing to answer them, relaxed and not standing in a doorway.

She ran to the tub like a cub being let out of the first time. Her legs sprang into action, as she approached the steps, and tossed the slippers she had on to the ground without hesitation. Fresh towels were laid out in case she wanted a dip.

She sank into the hot tub built for at least ten people even though we never had anyone up here, but us. "This is the life!"

In the past, we invited a visitor or two for the night to curb our sexual hunger, but never here to explore and enjoy the suite. She was the first one. I slowly peeled off my robe, and put it to the side, as she excitedly dipped her head in and laughed as the bubbles exploded around her body.

"Fagua, how did you know we were wolves? I assume you are not one?"

She shook her head, "I have the power of something. Pa would say of smell. Ma would say I have gifts. I don't know, I just knew. Sometimes. Well, not often…"

She stared at me, as if she wondered whether to talk to me or not about it. I nodded and her dark eyes beamed again. The same way when we first came to the hot tub.

"Sometimes, I see things." She swirled her hand over the surface of the bubbling water. "I never know if they're true. Like a dream, but I'm not sleeping, I'm wide awake. It's kind of weird, and in our town no one talks about it. Everyone pretends it doesn't exist, including my parents, and at the best of times including me."

"But you wanted to leave before, didn't you?"

She shook her head. "There was a feeling of entrapment I've always had about the town. I just used to think there was some spell over us. Several times I tried to leave on my own and always ended up going back before I crossed the border. It wasn't until Keith came that the spell was broken. I thought it was fate, you know, like we were meant to be together.

And forget about many visitors. We were surrounded by woods. It's easy for our wolves to shift and be in their other form. It's a little weird knowing there are wolves in the cities like you, Husk and Sky. Sometimes I feel as if it's the best and the worst kept secret. There's even a rumor about other types of shifters. I couldn't imagine that. Could you?"

I smiled, easing into the water across from her. "Well, I did come across a bear shifter once."

She laughed. "You're kidding?"

I chuckled, leaning back against the side. "Nope, but I'm pretty sure there are lions, bears, tigers. Heard a rumor of bee shifters too."

"Bees?"

I nodded. "Weird right."

"Definitely."

I couldn't think of anything else to say, because her breasts bounced in front of me from the hot tub jets. I had a hard time concentrating on just being in the tub and getting to know her better. The desire to take her was so strong I forced myself to resist, by staying where I was at the other side of the tub. I had to exercise control from the moment I'd seen her. I would have thought it would be easier by now. If anything, it was getting harder.

Yet, it was promising she was out here with me and not yelling or trying to escape. How long before she trusted us fully? Before she realized she was our mate?

"I need to get out. I'm getting tired. I think I need something to eat," she said as she brought me back to our reality, because I was lost in my thoughts.

"Sure, I'll whip you up something."

She laughed. "You cook?"

"Doesn't everyone in one form or another? Even Sky, who used to burn toast, can make a decent meal in the kitchen."

"Sorry, I didn't mean to offend you." She climbed out of the hot tub, pushing back her dark hair. "I just figured since you're rich and have all this, you wouldn't do simple tasks like cooking or cleaning."

"We didn't grow up rich. All of this you see has taken years of hard work and dedication."

She blushed.

"And a bit of luck." I climbed out of the hot tub and handed her a towel. "I was thinking later we could catch a new movie on the projector. How would you like to see the latest superhero movie?"

"Wait," she took the towel from me, wrapping it around her gorgeous body. "Not the one that's releasing soon?"

"The same." I dried off with the towel.

"Wow! They keep advertising it on TV. I never get to the movie theatre, and we don't even have one in town. I can't believe I'm going to see it. I haven't even seen the first one. But don't we have to wait till nightfall?" She waved a hand to the projector screen over the pool.

"Not at all. We have a theatre room with a projector indoors. We can watch it there. We could watch it again later and hit the swimming pool or watch something else."

"A girl could get used to this type of living," she said, adjusting her towel. "What about Husk and Sky? Will they be joining us?"

"They'll be back tomorrow, but that's no reason to enjoy the time we do have together."

"Where are they?"

I shrugged. "Business. We don't just stay here locked in the hotel forever. We do go out and have to meet suppliers and potential clients and guests."

"Makes sense, anyway, it's good. It means we can get to spend more time together." She smiled at me.

I really hoped she meant it. We would needed to take her out tomorrow and let her roam freely, then we'd see if she was really true to her word or if this was all an act to get us to lower our guard.

Maybe four days of self-isolation without putting any pressure on her had done the trick. Maybe for once in his life, Husk was better at handling and working with people than I was. I shook my head at the absurdity of the idea.

agua

Wrapped in the towel, I headed back to my room to take a quick shower. I thought about the question on my mind. It wasn't so much a question, but just a feeling. Did they lure me here?

I shook my head at the idea. No wolf would want their mate captured and then have her lay down with another. No, they were possessive, one thing for sure, and I was a virgin before I'd met Keith. At the time, knowing he wasn't a wolf made me want to have sex with him, since I knew I had the freedom of not being tied to him forever. And I guess the freedom of finally being somewhere other than my small town and drinking too much had warped my judgement.

All of this had to be a coincidence, and I had to stop being paranoid about it. The only thing I had to worry about was taking a quick shower and what to change into. Maybe I could get used to this type of life.

They wanted to take care of me, and all I'd done was complain and pout. It felt so easy with Winter, with him it didn't seem hard to relax and enjoy everything including his company. So natural in fact, unlike the other two.

Winter was tall and had the bluest eyes I'd ever seen. And I think when we were in the hot tub, he had a hard on. I stripped off my towel and wet swimsuit. As soon as the shower was warm enough, I stepped inside and imagined the streams of water going down my body being Winter's fingers touching me.

I wondered what it would be like to lay down with a wolf. The little I did know about them in the sack was it couldn't be called sex. My best friend told me about that part. She'd she said that her first and only time was magical. Nothing like being with a man, not that she had anything to compare. My virginity was more about losing it, because I felt as if I'd been holding on to it for too long, and with good reason. I had wanted to escape SmallHeath, and now I had. I couldn't think of anything better than going back with a wolf. Three. No, just one. Pa would be happy about that I was sure. He hated humans, and I guess part of me leaving with Keith was a little late rebellion. If Pa knew what he'd done, running off and leaving me here, he'd be more than happy to tell me he'd always told me humans were nothing but trouble.

"Are you going to stay in there forever or will you come out?" Winter asked, and I gasped.

I'd forgotten to lock my door.

"Coming," I shouted back, while putting the sponge between my legs, wishing it was his big, thick cock.

"Good, otherwise the food will be cold."

I didn't respond, as I continued to make myself come, not sure if I was ready to make a commitment to him, yet. It would take more than an afternoon in the tub and lunch. Yes, it would take a lot more than that.

CHAPTER 13

Winter

It was really weird, but when I knocked on her bedroom door, she said coming, and I couldn't help but wonder if she was touching herself in the shower.

No.

I didn't want to think that way, otherwise I wouldn't be able to control myself. My love for cooking kept all my sexual thoughts at bay. Sky and Husk will be back late this evening, and I wanted to spend as much time getting to know Fagua before they returned. The tension with them around was too much.

I went back into the kitchen and lightly heated up the steaks, then debated what to do about the Cuban rice I made. My phone chimed, but I ignored it, needing to get everything ready for Fagua. I knew the eggs would be cold, but then I could keep them at the same temperature in the oven. I rushed to do that, then felt satisfied she could take as long as she needed, as I decided to check the message.

You have the place to yourself. Sky and I are out for the night. H

I glanced at the work emails. I had so many damn ones unopened; too many, and I wished I'd never looked at my phone, because now I had the temptation to go through them.

Most of them should have been directed to Sky, and he should have been taking care of his shit. He'd been so damn unreliable lately, I shouldn't be surprised he'd let me down. Once again, I hated the idea of my brother losing it, but I couldn't hide the fact he'd been troubled. Maybe going out with Fagua would help him release some of the tension. I started shifting through all my emails, debating whether to send a message to Sky when she walked through the door.

She was breathtaking with her hair pinned up in a loose bun, strands of hair bouncing off her face as she approached me. I couldn't help but smile at her in the red strapless ruffle dress I'd bought, which hugged her body and emphasized her curves. I didn't care what Husk had said. She wasn't skin and bones to me. She was perfect, and as she came in closer, I smelled her perfume and the underlying scent of soap and the unique, addictive scent all her own. Between her beauty and the red, slinky dress, which made her pale skin light up, she was the most beautiful woman I'd ever seen. There was a slit up her thigh, and I forgot all about the time I'd been waiting for her.

"Sorry, I took so long," she said as she walked toward me like she was on a catwalk.

"You look absolutely beautiful," I confessed to her.

"No one's ever called me before." A little tear escaped her eye, and I felt guilty for ruining the perfection in front of me.

"So, what is this you made for us? I do like a man in the kitchen," She sniffled, her smile widening.

"I think all women do."

"True, but the men in our town, they're cavemen. They expect women to be in the kitchen, cooking and cleaning and in between breading cubs and having their legs wide open on the bed, and not necessarily in order."

I hated to break it to her, but it sounded like Husk in a nutshell. I removed the hot plates from the stove, and placed everything on the table, so I didn't have to get up and down. She talked freely, and it made me feel good knowing she felt comfortable enough with me.

"I've never been with anyone who makes me want to make an effort."

She surprised me with her open invitation, and I nearly dropped the steaks on the floor. She blushed and she turned away. I wanted her to tell me more, but then it was all too soon. I needed to make sure she was really ready, and one day, one night wouldn't mean she was ready for forever. And there was too much at stake to be playing games.

"The first dish is Cuban rice. Have you had it before?"

She shook her head.

"The next, well, it's kind of obvious, steak and salad and if you're hungry we can have ice-cream or cake for dessert. Would you care for some wine, or do you just want water?"

She laughed. "Are those the only two options?"

I couldn't help my grin. "No, there's more…"

"I'm just playing. I know, it was just kind of funny, the way you said it."

I sighed,"Sometimes, I think I'm taking after Husk. I get a little too serious at times."

"Oh no, don't. Please just be you. And I'll take wine, please."

I winked at her, "I'll try. Now, dig in before it gets cold again. I don't think I can reheat twice without ruining it. Afterward we'll catch the movie in the theatre and see where the night takes us."

She raised her empty glass, and I quickly filled it with the cabernet sauvignon and did the same for my own.

I lifted my glass in a toast. "Sounds like a plan!"

We clinked glasses and she took a big sip before tasting all the food. Her moans while she ate had my cock hardening.

"Husk and Sky are going to be sorry they

missed this," she said between bites. "I feel sorry for Sky, but Husk needs to be taken down a notch anyway."

I didn't want her to be thinking of Husk as the big, bad wolf. They were changing, so fast. I was worried my plan wouldn't work. She didn't know what was at stake, and I wasn't about to tell her. She had to surrender to us, and I didn't want her to think it was forced. She had to do it willingly, and I had to keep myself under control, to make sure I didn't lose it completely.

agua

I had the feeling I embarrassed myself by admitting to Winter I wanted him. It'd been the first time we'd had a conversation, and here I was declaring he could take me.

Except I wasn't teasing him. I meant every word, and I'd been plucking up the courage to tell him I wanted to stay with him. Not his brothers, but him.

"Are you ready to watch the movie?" He sat down next to me with a big bowl of popcorn he'd made. I felt as if I were in the movie theatre for the first time. He'd also brought a little wine to make me feel relaxed, but I didn't need the wine. I'd already drank some earlier, and I wasn't much of a drinker. Back home, we only had it on special occasions. It felt silly to say that to him, after all I was twenty-five, dressed like a lady, and I wanted him to see me as one, not the naive country bumpkin hiding inside of me right now.

"What is it?"

I shook my head, as I lied about the idea of this being something I was used to doing.

"Nothing. I just wondered if you'd left. If being alone in the dark with me had scared you?"

The movie flashed on, and he was distracted for a second, but then he whispered in my ear.

"One step at a time, I don't want you to do anything, you don't want to do. I want us to get to know each other better."

I looked at him, wondering if I'd gotten him all wrong. Wolves didn't work like that, but then again what did I really know about how they worked? Whenever Rebecca tried to tell me and even my Ma, I stopped her. I pretended as if any problems didn't exist, and now I wished I'd listened, because I didn't want to confess the truth to him. I'd given him the idea I was confident and knew exactly what I was doing, but I didn't. He would figure it out.

"I only know about your scent and nothing else."

He winked. "Good. Enjoy the movie."

His reaction should have made me nervous, but he had a way of making me feel as if I could believe anything he said, and I knew it would be okay as he held my hand while we watched the movie together. If Winter wasn't with me, then I would have had the hots for the sexy actor who played Ironman like every woman on and off screen. This guy had nothing in comparison to Winter, because I had more than a man sitting next to me, and I wanted to please him in more ways than one.

"Did you enjoy the movie?"

I jumped up, knocking the empty popcorn bowl on the floor, and I hugged him. He'd given me an experience I could never forget, and one I would cherish for the rest of my days.

He swept me in his arms and held on to me. The lights switched on as the credits came to an end, and it was as if he waited for this moment to take me.

He grabbed my face with both hands and looked me deep in the eyes. My breath caught, but I smiled to give him the permission to take me. He could do whatever he pleased. He shoved his lips to mine. I closed my eyes as his mouth explored mine skillfully. His hands no longer held my face, but one hand rested on my back for support, whereas the other explored my body.

I responded with pleasure. I felt the hunger inside him, in his kiss like it was threatened to catch us both on fire. His hand moved down to my breasts and nipples, rubbing and stroking me. Deep in my core, there began a burning sensation. I moaned into his mouth. I wanted more than mere petting like I'd done before. He responded with a growl, amping up the sexual tension between us even more.

I started to pant as I wanted to rip my dress off and have him do things to me I know were nowhere near what Keith would have done. I felt the desire between the two of us, knowing in a snap of his fingers, he could tear my dress to threads.

He swiftly moved his hand from my breasts. My nipples were erect, and the need for him to suck on them ached through me so badly I wanted to scream. I let go of the seat and held onto him. Every part of me shook, and with my powers it extended even the theatre. I felt the vibrations through the floor and my seat, but I couldn't stop. Winter made me feel too good to care.

He dipped his hand up my dress, and the thong snapped me when he ripped it off.

"Ouch," I cried out.

"Did I hurt you?"

"Don't stop," I pleaded.

His hand smoothed along my leg and brushed over my clit. I gasped, clinging to him and kissing him. He plunged two fingers into me.

"You're so wet!"

He didn't wait for a response as he drove his tongue back into my mouth and started to slowly move his fingers in and out of me. I moved with the rhythm of his fingers. What he was doing to me felt so good, so right. I didn't want him to stop.

I want to take off my dress and feel his cock, against my leg. The promise of things to come was too much to bear as I tried to move.

He held on to me and growled. "There's no rush. No one's coming to find us. I want to take my time."

I grabbed his thick arms, wanting to feel his body next to mine, as the heat in the room overcame me, and I started to sweat. My breath became faster and heavier as the friction of his fingers sent me into overdrive.

He curled his fingers and hit my G-spot.

"Fuck!" I screamed out as the orgasm was building, then exploded as I came on his fingers.

I opened my eyes, and he watched me as I screamed my pleasure.

"Come with me," He commanded as he switched places, so I no longer lay on his lap, but faced him, and his cock pushed against his pants, thrusting against my sex.

He started to rub me up and down against

his erection, controlling my movement, making me, loose myself in the sensation.

His hand moved to my dress, as he tugged it down and ripped it at the seams. It was as if Winter wanted to come too, as he started to make even more animal noises as he rocked me harder towards him.

I wondered if his cock had come out of his pants, but then I couldn't look. I couldn't do anything as the mother of all orgasms made me scream at the top of my lungs.

"Yes, yes, yes," I panted as I shook uncontrollably, and Winter loosened his once tight grip.

He held me gently in his arms, and I could feel his cock jerking like a gun, as his cum started to seep through his pants.

I smiled, as we were both breathless, and finally, I could open my eyes again.

"Did you enjoy that?"

I laughed. "So much but we could have gone to the bedroom or..."

He lifted his finger against my lips, and I smelled my juices on his fingers. I was so tempted to lick it, but he said, "All good things come to those who wait. I didn't mean to lose control. I'm sorry."

I shook my head. "No. I thought you didn't want me. You haven't made a move all day, and I know you wanted to."

He stroked my hair, as if he admired my beauty, and there was something in the way he touched me which made me feel comfortable with my decision. I was thinking I was in way over my head, but being with him today made me confident about life with him. I hadn't ever felt this way with anyone.

"I didn't want to rush you." Winter tucked my hair behind my ears, staring at me. "We've only spent one day together. I need you to be comfortable with the decision you make when you make it."

I shook my head. "What if I want you to claim me?" I couldn't believe I'd spoken out loud. I hadn't even gotten divorced from Keith yet. Maybe the wine had lowered my inhibitions too much. I started to pull away, embarrassed, but Winter held onto me.

He smiled. "It doesn't work like that. We all have to claim you. Not just me."

It was the answer I thought he would say,

and I tried to hide my disappointment by not looking him in the eyes, but turning my head away.

"Besides you must be tired. You've been working overtime."

"Sorry?"

He nodded towards the projector and the seats in the theatre, some of them were at the opposite side of the room, the projector was broken.

"Oh sorry," I whispered. I'd totally lost control of my powers. I licked my lips. "I thought my curse only worked in SmallHeath and nowhere else, you must be drawing them out."

He lifted me up and headed towards the door. Cradled in his arms, he stepped over a lot of the damage. Broken chairs and ripped up carpet. There was so much more damage than I had realized. Embarrassed, I covered my face.

"It's not a curse. It's a gift." Winter kissed my forehead. "Who told you it only worked in SmallHeath?"

"Ma did, that's why she said as much as I wanted to leave, I never should."

He paused as he reached the door, and he

kicked it open. "You're tired Fagua, get some rest, and we'll talk in the morning."

I noticed his scent had changed, maybe it was my imagination, but before he'd smelled so old, and now so young.

"Is it late?"

He shook his head, and I held on to him so tightly. I loved being in his arms and being carried to my room. I wanted him to lay down with me, but I knew it wasn't an option. He'd already stated they all needed to claim me, and he knew I wasn't willing to give myself to Husk, but then again the feeling seemed more than mutual.

In my room, he laid me on the bed like a delicate flower and kissed my cheek. "Get to some rest."

In one swift movement, he tore off the rest of my dress and stared at me for a few seconds. My skin flushed thinking he was debating joining me or not. I was naked, even my strapless bra had been miraculously torn off as he'd brought me to climax earlier. His once limp cock rose to life again, tenting his pants. "Sweet dreams."

When he left me alone, disappointment sank into my chest.

I had a feeling he wouldn't have good dreams because he'd left himself frustrated. I didn't want to be with his brothers, only him. Maybe in time, he would see that, but did I really want to come between Winter and his brothers?

CHAPTER 15

Husk

"Doc, how's Sky doing?" I asked as soon as he came out of the room, and I knew it was bad news from the way his shoulders slumped slightly and the tension around his brown eyes.

Doc was a lot smaller, and at first when we met him, we didn't think he was a wolf. It was unusual for someone so short, and small in frame, to be a wolf. Now we knew many of our kind.

He shook his head. "He's so fucking weak,

I've never seen him like this. How are you feeling?"

I wanted to lie and tell him I was feeling okay. But, he scanned me with his eyes narrowing as if he knew the answer to his own question. I'd eaten seven times today, and each time food hit my mouth and down my throat, it made me feel a little bit stronger for a few minutes. Just a few, and then I would feel the need to eat again.

"Not great. But not as bad as Sky. Has he fully shifted?"

He shook his head.

"I've never seen him like this, only half of his body has shifted and the other half, well thank fuck it was still in human form, or I couldn't have got him out of the office in time."

Doc patted my back, as he moved his glasses. He pinched the bridge of his nose and stepped back shaking his head.

"How's Winter doing?"

"Fine. He's watching over Fagua right now." And a flash of jealousy hot and fast drove into my stomach. Which didn't make any sense because I knew she hated me, and I wasn't enamored with her either after her little attitude at lunch days ago.

His eyes lit up. "So, it's true. The seer was right, there is a mate, and she can cure you all. This is excellent news, why didn't you tell me you had found her?"

I nodded, thinking he was more excited about us finding her than I was at the moment.

"Yes, I thank you for putting us in contact with the seer."

He was good to us, just like our father had told us he would be.

I cleared my throat trying to find ways to express myself, as my mind flashed for a split second to my parents who had died too young in the tragic car accident.

"This is good news, I mean if it's true, then why did you bring him here?" He replaced his glasses. "Why not take him home so she could heal him?"

I looked down at the floor, embarrassed to admit our mate was more scared of me, rather than willing to lay down with me. I knew I had to stay away tonight, just so Winter could get her out of the room.

"I see." He scratched his balding head, and I

forgot for a second he had the power to read minds. I hated when he did it, especially without permission. I crossed my arms and a warning growl broke through me.

"Sorry Husk." He could tell his intrusion had rubbed me the wrong way. "It's just as I get older and weaker, I forget myself at times. I don't even feel comfortable looking after Sky. My powers and strength are not the same as they used to be."

I nodded as I sat down next to him on the bench.

"I have to go to L.A. tomorrow, to tend to another." He sighed. "Do you think you could stay here with Sky?"

"What about the nurse and staff?"

He shook his head. "It's getting worse, and they left in search of their mates. They couldn't stay here. Their fate would be like mine and they know our kind are dying and with no mate, there's no life."

I hated the fact Doc was only one year older than me. He looked as if there was at least a twenty-year age gap, because it was too late for him.

"You could find a mate if you wanted to,

just like them. You don't need to sacrifice your-self and stay just to help the remainder of us."

He coughed. "I could, but I could die trying; besides my true mate was killed by another wolf. I've tried to get over it, but over the years it's just made me bitter about what our kind have become. Before, we used to be clans who respected each other, now it's as if we're every wolf for themselves."

We sat in silence. I thought about my parents and what the greed of our kind had done to them, resulting in their deaths.

Doc cleared his throat. "I'm happy you have found her. You need to do what you can to keep her, or you'll suffer the same fate as Sky, or worse. I would hate for you to do that, but I think you need to bring her here and start the healing process, the quicker the better," he said as he patted my leg.

He stood like he was about to leave me, but I had to get everything off my chest, and he felt like the only person I could talk to about anything right now who would understand.

"Sky shifted not so long ago, but why has he been hit worse? None of this makes sense, Winter and I always thought he would never shift. We'd hoped, but his body is like it's trying to rip him apart."

Doc nodded "I know, but you've been living with it for years. Sometimes the mind plays tricks on us, and mixed with his unhealthy appetite for drinking, it hasn't helped him at all. I need to get ready for L.A. Anything you need, don't hesitate to call me."

He flashed away before I could say anything else. His second power of teleportation was too handy. My power felt insignificant compared to his, but he was right. I had to get Fagua here and get her to help Sky. Winter, hopefully, would have connected with her, and her being reasonable would be appreciated right now. I couldn't deal with her being difficult or having to deal with any matters of the heart.

Winter

It'd been two days since Sky and Husk had done their disappearing act. However, their presence wasn't missed as Fagua and I spent time together. It felt like we were on honeymoon, and there was no pressure on my side for her to commit to us. We'd talked about taking it to the next level, but I couldn't break away from my brothers, and I had to be honest with her, too. Everything was going in the right direction so far. I'd slept better than I had for weeks. Yet my wolf instincts told me Sky and Husk were not doing so well.

"What's the plan for today?" Fagua asked as she walked into my bedroom. She was busy trying to seduce me. Se'd made it clear in the movie theatre she wanted me.

I lifted the covers and showed her I was ready for her.

She smiled as she walked towards me. Every single movement was slow and careful. It was as if she waited for me to reject her. I wasn't going to do that, not today, not ever if I could help it.

She crawled onto the bed and leaned over me. I pressed my hand gently into her lower back as she bent over me, before sliding my palm down, and resting on the curve of her ass.

"Do you really want to do this?"

I asked for confirmation, as her pussy was only an inch or less away from my rising cock.

Every muscle in her body tensed as she closed her eyes and whispered, "Yes."

Her nipples hardened, and she clenched her jaw as if she prepared herself for the journey we were both about to undertake. It wasn't just about having sex, or even lust. There was so much more at stake, and she needed to understand by claiming and mating with her, we were going to bond just not for this morning but forever.

I heard her heart pounding in her chest. The sound of it made me know she was nervous and excited about what was to come. I trailed my hand down her thighs, gently caressing her flesh, and admiring the beauty of her body. I wanted her to look me in the eyes and confirm she knew what we were going to do.

"Lie on the bed," I broke the silence as I moved her to the side of me. I wanted to appreciate every inch of her.

Without any hesitation she did what I said. My hands traced every part of her, memorizing her curves and shape. Not one part of her body was left untouched.

She purred. "Mmm..." Confirming she loved every caress, and she arched her back on the bed.

I moved over her and soon replaced my hands with gentle kisses from her face right down to her toes. I used my hands as a guide as I spread my fingertips and brushed the softness of her skin. She watched me intently. Her skin flushed, and her scent grew addictive.

Her chest rose and fell with each breath as I moved in between her legs. I wanted to kiss her sweet pussy, longing for a taste of it. I kissed the top of her thighs, moving closer to her pussy. I flicked my tongue down the length of her folds, and she sucked in a strong breath.

"Are you ready for me to take you?"

I slid my fingers inside her, coating them with her juices.

Her moans grew louder as I pumped my fingers in and out of her. My mouth kissed her clit.

"You're so damn wet. It's like a river pouring out of you." I growled, as my tongue replaced my fingers, and I started to lick her, deep enough not to miss an inch of her.

"Fuck! Yes!" Her screams filled the room.

From the short time I'd known and spent with her, she wasn't one for cursing. She was more of a "dammit!" or "holy cow!" kind of girl. Now she ripped through all those words and the bed started to shake. It turned me on even more, as I flicked my tongue, piercing her gently.

I used my arms to steady the bed, and my knees to push down on the mattress. Everything around us was moving, apart from the bed.

She screamed even louder, and I knew she was coming to the edge. Her body started to rise into the air and I used my hands to hold her firmly down.

I couldn't hold back any longer. I swiftly moved on top of her and our eyes met. It was then she was aware of her surroundings as if I'd brought her back down to reality as my cock teased the entrance of her pussy.

"Control your emotions. Let me take you. Enjoy it. Don't fight it."

She nodded, and I moved inside her. I didn't want to rip her sweet pussy. Every time, I went a little deeper her hands clutched my back, her nails digging in even deeper. She was ready for me. I kissed her mouth, darting my tongue past her lips.

She didn't hold back as she kept one hand on my shoulder and the other at the back of my head. I moved in deeper, holding her tightly as my cock completely filled her. I expected her to scream, or tell me it was too much, but she held onto me tightly. The chaos that was happening in the room came to a dramatic halt. I knew then she was relaxed, as she started to moan into my mouth. I picked up the pace, building the rhythm slightly as I didn't want this moment to end. I'd been waiting and holding back for far too long to cum inside of her. No, it had to go on for as long as possible.

No more was I holding back as the heat of our bodies started combine, not only was she wet down there. My fantasies of what it would be like to be inside of her were nothing compared to the real thing. She felt like heaven. As she held onto me, as my body stroked hers, we now moved to the same rhythm.

Her pussy enveloped my cock as if it were made for it. I'd never been inside of a human fully, not like this. No woman coupled ever withstood the pain, but not Fagua. She wasn't any ordinary human.

She was my mate. She was mine.

I wanted every piece of her, morning, noon and night. The idea of sharing her with my brothers cast out of my mind. I stopped holding back, and my cum rose from inside of me.

I moved faster, jerking uncontrollably as I couldn't continue to kiss her. No, I couldn't even fuck her mouth with my tongue, as my sperm exploded out of my cock and into her. I didn't know how deep it went, but it felt as if it went on for a few seconds as I tried to move away from her to catch my breath, yet it just went on and on.

When my climax finally came to an end, I flopped on top of her.

"That was so intense," she whispered as she struggled to breathe.

I quickly jumped up away from her, worried I'd nearly crushed her to death with my weight.

"You okay?"

She laughed. "Yeah, you are a bit heavy. I never noticed until just now."

As I slid onto the side, I drew her into my arms. She curled up next to me. It was the best feeling ever. My cock had other ideas as it started to come back to life with her ass pressed against my groin.

"You're not tired?" she asked.

"You are so we'll wait." I kissed her lightly

along her neck and shoulder. "I don't want to break you just as soon as we've started."

"Winter, you really think I'm fragile? Like a porcelain doll you don't want to break."

I shook my head, as she pulled away from me and I drew her near.

"No."

She was right, I was too gentle with her. She was tougher than I'd given her credit for, but then as my gaze danced around the room. The mirror over the dresser was broken, clothes littered the floor, and parts of the ceiling were ripped off. Even the damn door hung by the hinges. Yeah, I hadn't given her enough credit. She was tough, a lot tougher.

$\mathcal{H}$usk

I couldn't wait around anymore, so I headed back home. Sky appeared a little stronger, not a lot, but enough where he could have a short conversation. As for the casino, it seemed to be running itself because when I went to the office, our assistant pointed out she hadn't seen Winter for three days. He'd left instructions for everyone to carry on as usual, and there was a reason why he'd done it. He'd told Hayley if things couldn't run without him, then there was no reason for him to hire anyone. It was an arrogant statement, even if there was some truth behind it. We didn't hire staff to do our jobs. I didn't expect him to not come in at all. Had he been so blinded by Fagua he'd lost all his senses?

I stormed into the elevator and went to our suite. All the furniture was turned over with several chairs broken apart and lying in a heap. Both Lourdes and Maria pushed the sofa back.

"What happened here?" I yelled.

"We don't know. We just came to clean and saw the place like this."

"Leave it," I barked.

"But sir, we've been trying to put everything back," Lourdes said.

I glared at her for questioning me, and she held her head down, walking away. She knew better than to try and reason with me, especially when I was in this mood. She'd been working for us for over five years. She was our housekeeper and knew our secret. The reason we hired her in the first place was because she'd been raised by wolves. We didn't know why she'd left her clan or what had happened, but it was a case of we didn't ask any questions and neither did she.

She could keep her mouth shut, something

which was valued in our business. We didn't need anyone finding out our secrets. Wolves kept to themselves, and outsiders, especially humans, got antsy whenever they'd found out the truth about shifters in the past. It never worked out for either side. We needed loyalty, and Lourdes had it in spades.

On my way to Winter's room I stopped in my tracks in the hallway. The whole place looked like someone had unleashed a tornado. I had to weave past objects from the kitchen, such as the microwave which was now in the hallway.

"What the fuck?" I growled once I was outside Winter's door.

Muffled noises and a bed squeaking in rhythm had me clenching my fists. They were acting as if they were on their fucking honeymoon.

"Oh, god, Winter," Fagua's shout echoed through the door. "Yes, yes."

The walls vibrated and cracks shot up from the floor to the ceiling.

It was as if they were in their own world, and they didn't care about the mess they'd created as they were doing it. Disappointment at my brother's reaction to being with her clouded my mind filled with rage at Fagua. She'd been with Keith, maybe not sexually, but he'd touched her, and done a lot more than given her a goodnight kiss on the cheek. Why else would she leave town to marry him within a week? I didn't know all the details, but then again, I didn't need to.

What made me even more mad was the fact we hadn't seen Winter for three damn days. He'd called a couple of times, the first day, but then as soon as I sent the text, saying we were held up, he'd forgotten about us.

His own brothers. With Sky in the hospital and dealing with a partial shift and the curse.

It was as if Fagua had made Winter forget us. I could have waited patiently for them to finish their little rendezvous, but I didn't hesitate as I stormed inside. The door blew back against the wall and I growled.

"Winter, in my room now."

I stared at the crown molding, broken in hunks along the ceiling. I didn't want to see her body, or even his in any type of position. It'd be a memory I wouldn't be able to erase. I didn't wait for a response, as I left with the same haste in which I entered the room.

I thought for a second Winter had said no. If he wasn't here in two minutes, I was going to haul his naked ass out pronto. But there's no way he'd defy me, his older brother. I shook off my paranoia and went to see if the bar in the corner of the living room was still standing for a fucking drink. I didn't need just a shot of something to make me feel better. No, I needed the whole fucking bottle.

"So, you decide to show up?" Winter asked as he caught me sitting on the now righted couch and staring at the bottle.

I needed to get rid of my bad habits like. Seeing the bottle in front of me, my mind drifted to Sky. If he were here, he would be reaching for it. Then again, if we were going to die soon, what was the point of worrying about giving up smoking or anything?

"Really? We've been out and all you can do is…"

"Mate!" He smiled coming closer and sitting on the arm of the couch next to me. He had no shirt or shoes. He was dressed as if he were in the Bahamas with linen pants, topless, and his toes stretched out as if he felt sand at the bottom of his feet. Didn't think I'd ever seen Winter dressed so casually. He always dressed like a damn prep-school guy or in a three-piece suit even on our days off. As though sensing my anger, he stood, pacing toward the patio window across from me. He crossed his arms and face me, his chin high.

"If you and Sky wanted to come home then you could…"

"Shut the fuck up." I couldn't listen to him anymore or I would do something I would regret. I stood and moved closer to him because I wanted him to hear and understand everything I had to say. I drew out the cigar I'd been saving and pointed it at him.

"Sky is dying. I've been in the hospital trying to see if there was another way. Something to make him better, but there's nothing."

He shook his head, then jerked the cigar I was about to light up on the floor.

"Dying? And you just felt the need to tell me

now." He shoved me backward with a fist into my shoulder. "What the fuck, Husk? Whatever your problem is with Fagua, you need to get rid of it. We brought her here to help us, not to tear us apart."

I chuckled. "Is why you've been fucking her for the last few days?"

My blood boiled, my veins popping as I wanted to do something to my brother. Something I'd never felt before. Sure, we argued. Raged. But to physically hurt each other, it had only started when she'd come into our lives, Rage began to take over as Winter stared at me, challenging me to hit him, or even worse, fight him.

"What do we need to do?" Winter said.

I caught my breath and tried to calm down.

"No, what do I need to do?" Fagua said, coming around the corner.

I wondered how long she'd been out there listening, but we didn't have time to discuss the possibility.

"You need to mate with him," Winter commanded as I moved towards her.

She stood wearing only a white silk bathe robe, the smell of sex lingering in the air, "No. I can't just mate with him like that. I'm not some kind of robot goes around sleeping with wolves."

"It didn't stop you fucking Winter!" Shit, I knew I had blown any chance of getting her on our side the moment the words escaped my mouth. I regretted them immediately. Winter shot me a look, as if to say, "you've gone and done it again". As for Fagua, she stormed out of the room. I couldn't believe our plan was falling apart when we'd spent so much time getting her in the first place.

"This is your mess. You go fix it. I'm going to the office. One of us has to work around here."

With that, I left Winter in the room standing there and looking lost.

When I looked over my shoulder, he scratched his head. I had a feeling their mating had nothing to do with us, and only to do with him. Fagua was more dangerous than I'd imagined. Somewhere along the line she managed to divide us, something which had never happened until now. Our mate was our destroyer. She wasn't bringing us together, but rather ripping us apart.

agua

No fucking way!

The deal was thirty days, not to fuck the whole damn family. No, they said they wanted me to stay, and now they had me under pressure. Husk, I couldn't stand him. The guy was so damn creepy. The way he talked and demanded everything, not like he owned the casino, but the whole damn world. As for Sky, we hadn't exchanged more than pass me the salt at the dinner table, and even then, Husk had made me go to my room.

The only one out of the three who'd showed

me any kindness from the moment I had been told to stay was Winter. This was why we mated, and why I want him and him alone. I shook my head at the idea of mating all three of them.

"No, no and no!" I said to myself once I got into my room and looked for shoes and clothing, so I could get out of here. Not just the rooftop, but I felt the need to get as far away from the casino as possible.

At some point when I'd been with Winter, the staff had washed and put away all the new clothes and shoes into one of my closets. I found some brand new sneakers. After dressing in a pair of shorts and a blouse that hugged my breasts, and I put the shoes on too. I smoothed my hair down and reached the door. Winter stood there, looking at me.

"I need to be alone." I crossed my arms.

"I can see." He moved out of the way.

I felt bad for him. His brother was dying, and I seemed to be the answer. The crazy thought which popped into my head once, reappeared again. This wasn't a coincidence. I hadn't been sold; they had brought me here for this reason.

"Tell me one thing." I lifted my chin as I stared into Winter's sapphire eyes and dared him to lie to me. "Did Keith really owe you guys money, or you just wanted me here?"

He cleared his throat as if he thought about his response.

"Both. He owed us money, and we wanted you here."

Before we'd mated, Winter had smelled like an old man, approaching death. Now, it seemed he was young again. Has being with me changed him?

"So, all this was some sort of trap." I threw my hands into the air and stomped forward, pressing a finger into his chest. "You used me. Am I some sort of healing machine or something? You needed me to live. Is all I am to you?"

He shook his head. "No, it wasn't a trap. You're free to go. It's just not simple. I don't even know how to explain it all to you. And the mood you're in, I can tell you're not willing to listen. Look, I need to go see Sky."

Then his gaze shifted to the carpet, and he walked away. He wouldn't stop me, but then he also didn't answer my questions.

What did this all mean?

Did it mean Keith had lured me here and this was the reason why I had to mate with them?

Shit, of course.

I couldn't trust them.

Once again, I'd been deceived. It was as if everyone I'd ever met wanted to deceive me. I couldn't believe I'd been so dumb to fall for all of this, which was probably why I only graduated high school and never furthered my education. I was too dumb to study or do anything with my life.

I didn't know who I hated more.

Winter for using me, or Keith for selling me to them like some piece of trash. They lived in a penthouse, had money at their feet, and yet they did nothing to enjoy it.

I turned around, facing the empty suite. As much as I wanted to leave, I had no money. I couldn't go back home. Everything about my life felt like one big lie. I couldn't trust anyone, no one at all. The question would be if I would come back. Right now I didn't feel like it. I'd been used and there was nothing worse than this feeling pressing in on my chest, making it hard to breathe.

I shoved whatever I could find in my case and headed out. I checked my purse. I had a hundred dollars and not a lot on my credit card. I couldn't get far on the little money I had, but I had to leave.

I couldn't stay here. Everything about me was changing, I'd gone from being able to move a small, silver vase in SmallHeath to moving objects in a room. The whole thing was crazy. This place wasn't good for my health. It felt toxic.

I headed down the empty hallway. I stopped in my tracks as Lourdes smiled at me, then carried on putting broken objects in the bin.

I wanted to ask her if I'd done that?

I couldn't speak as I'd decided to leave. Nothing and no one could stop me, including the triplets. I snorted at my own joke as the three brothers couldn't be more different.

My heart squeezed as I thought about Winter losing his brother. I should at least say good-bye. I shook my head. He should have told me the truth. He had plenty of time, but he chose not to.

He'd taken my virginity and made me feel special. Tears formed in my eyes as reality weighed heavy on my heart. I thought I meant something to him. But he'd used me. I guess, everyone uses everyone. I'd used Keith to leave SmallHeath, and he'd used me to pay his debts.

No matter how it felt as if my heart was breaking, I had to leave. There was no turning back now. The elevator doors opened. I raised my head high and entered. Did the elevator have a sensor or something? I didn't remember pressing the button. The last time I tried to leave, Husk told me I needed a key. Now with the doors wide open, I walked in and the button for the ground floor flashed. I looked up at Winter standing outside the elevator.

I avoided his stare, but I couldn't get the elevator doors to close. He just stood watching me, as if he couldn't take his eyes off me, but he couldn't tell me to stay either.

CHAPTER 19

agua

I had a suitcase crammed full of clothes I'd never possessed in my life, and all I could think about was how to get out of this town. Everything that had happened in the space of two weeks had made me feel degraded. I got out of the elevator and kept walking, and walking, not knowing what direction I was going in, or even what I was doing, but walking seemed to solve my problems.

Downtown was confusing, and I felt like I'd been walking in circles. A big clock chimed, confirming I'd been walking for over two hours. I'd never walked so far in my life. It was as if my anxiety was going into overtime, and the more I walked, the more it relaxed me until I was hungry.

I stumbled across a diner, which was pretty quiet, and I strolled inside, dragging my case with me. I was a healer. This must be why Pa didn't want me to leave town. He wanted me to stay and heal the wolves. So many damn thoughts ran through my mind. Like Winter and why he and his brothers had lured me here in the first place. They had made out like Keith was the jerk, but he wasn't, not entirely. Maybe he had been the innocent one after all.

So many damn questions and no answers.

I slumped into the empty booth, thinking I didn't even have to read the menu to know I craved every scent that was teasing my nose right now, from pancakes to greasy hamburgers. At this rate, the hundred dollars I had in my purse would be spent today.

"You look as if you could do with something stronger than anything we serve here," the pretty blonde server said.

I blinked my eyes for a second, wondering

if it was Ma in front of me. They appeared to be the same age, and even had the same pointy, sharp nose and sparkling blue eyes.

"No." I shook my head to clear it. "Just whatever your special is, I could do with something to eat. I haven't eaten for a while."

She winked. "Leave it to me. I know just what you need."

I chuckled, thinking she did not know what all I'd been through. It didn't take her long to come back with coffee and a big hamburger with all the trimmings. I laughed for a split second about the guys being here. I had a quick vision of Husk demanding he wanted four more of them. The pile of fries around the burger were still steaming, and I couldn't wait to dig into everything. I doused the fries with salt and pepper then wondered if one of the guys liked them this way too, or if they'd grumble I'd ruined them, or maybe drown them in ketchup.

I shook my head at the idea. They were the last people I should think about.

"Hopefully, this will put a smile on your face." The server left a giant chocolate piece of cake complete with whipped cream and chocolate sprinkles on top.

As I ate my mind didn't wonder. The food was so good, and I was so starved I ate it all, even licked the whipped cream off my fork.

I noticed a guy looking at me. I turned my head away because I didn't want to give him the wrong idea. But he stepped up to me and hovered over my table. I finished the last bite, and I closed my eyes for a split second to savor the taste and ignore him. He was a middle-aged man with an oversized belly and a balding head, which he tried to disguise with his fading baseball cap. I knew it, before he even lifted the hat off his head by the way it sat so low on his head and no hair poked out anywhere. There were so many truckers like him, humans who stopped in at our diner. It was rare, but enough for me to know he must be one of those guys.

"Agua right?" He pointed at me.

"No. Fagua."

So he knew me.

"Sorry, I didn't mean to stare and scare you. It's just I recognized you and couldn't remember your name. Your parents own the diner and pretty much everything in Small-Heath. I've stopped over there twice."

I motioned for him to sit because he seemed nervous just standing in front of me.

"Not nearly everything in town. But, yeah they own the diner and the factory."

"And the bar and the store."

I nodded in agreement. "Yeah, they did, but I hardly go in there so sometimes, I just don't think about it."

"Well, there's not much else in SmallHeath."

That we could agree on.

"Anyway, I've taken up enough of your time and you have to have the berry pie too. It's worth dying for. I need to be heading back on the road."

It was as if the last part of his sentence gave me an idea.

"Where are you heading?"

He sat down. This was when it hit me. Like so many truckers, they were on the road all the time, and when they came into the diner, they loved to talk. It was a lonely job; it paid well but still lonely.

"I'm not going to SmallHeath, but I could get you near there. If you like?"

I nodded. Home. Where else could I go? Ma and Pa would be so angry I'd left, but relieved I was okay. And I had questions for them, like why they'd never told me about this apparent healing ability I had. At the thought, my gut clenched with remorse of leaving Sky when he was dying. No, that couldn't be true. It had to be another lie Husk had thought up to try and keep me trapped there.

"I gather you came to see the bright lights, and it wasn't all it cracked up to be."

"Something like that." I shrugged.

"I have to get a few things, then I could meet you back here in about twenty minutes. Sound good?" He shot to his feet, as if the idea of us traveling together was a bonus for him. He didn't realize he was helping me out, in more ways than one.

"You've got a deal." I smiled at him.

He ducked his head, and as quick as he was by my side, he was out of it again.

"Are you sure honey, going with Frank?" My server came up to me with the check. "I mean he seems nice and all, but a pretty young thing like you, needs to be careful."

She was worried about my safety, but she

didn't have to be. Besides I sensed underneath his gruff appearance, he had a big cuddly exterior. Frank seemed to be a nice guy.

"Seems to be a nice guy, and I could really do with the ride."

She put a gentle hand on my shoulder. "Be careful."

I was about to say something to reassure her, but before I got the chance some rude customers complained about their food and let everyone know they had an issue with their order. I hated people like that. I'd come across them one too many times at the diner. They didn't have issues with their orders, but whatever problems they had in their lives. Without a care for anyone else but themselves, they decided they needed to take it out on their server. As if we were really the one causing their bad day.

When she returned, I asked for two pieces of the berry pie to go. One small way I could pay Frank back for taking me back close to home.

As soon as she brought the pies, I tucked them to my chest. I felt better already, the feeling of a good meal had satisfied me so much and the kindness of the server made me forget for the time while I was in here.

"Thank you." I took a note of the server name—Wendy—and the address.

Outside, Frank waited at the door. It was time to go home and face the music. I knew it was going to be a long drive. We had over sixteen hundred miles to travel. I had to think about what I would say, the parts I would tell my parents and the others I'd leave out. Either way, I knew once I got there, they'd make it difficult, seeing as I left and didn't have the courage to tell them to their faces, but had left a note.

"Ready?" Frank asked as I pushed open the door.

"Uh-huh."

"I picked up some things, you know, in case you get hungry on the way. Some nuts, water and pretty much extras of everything I usually take on a trip. Hope that's okay?"

"Here." I handed him one of the pieces of pie. "Did you bring some extra bottles of beer?" I knew there was no way they didn't drink on the road.

"I didn't think you were a beer kinda gal. But you can share mine."

"Thanks." I didn't want him to feel guilty about not buying any for me. Especially seeing as he'd been so considerate and brought things for me to snack on, during the trip.

"Great. Let's get out of here."

Frank's gestures and words made me realize my first instinct was right, even if it wasn't about the wolves or Keith. Frank was a gentle giant, and he'd proved I was right. I just had to worry about what to say to my parents. For sure that would be the hardest part.

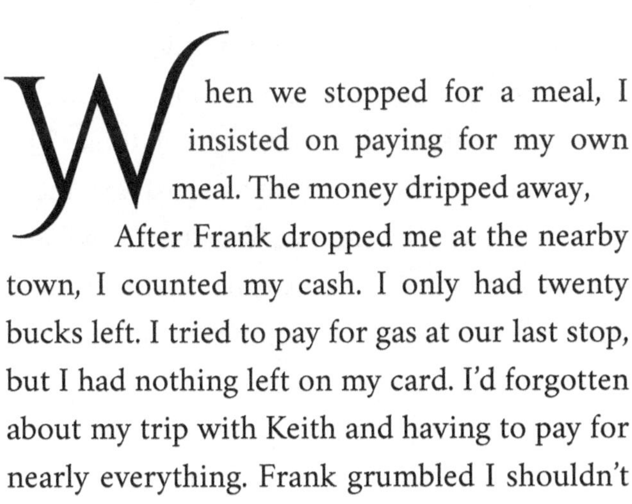

When we stopped for a meal, I insisted on paying for my own meal. The money dripped away, After Frank dropped me at the nearby town, I counted my cash. I only had twenty bucks left. I tried to pay for gas at our last stop, but I had nothing left on my card. I'd forgotten about my trip with Keith and having to pay for nearly everything. Frank grumbled I shouldn't pay for anything, but it still made me feel so guilty I couldn't even do much for him.

I lied when Frank dropped me. I had said I could get on the bus. I waved to him at the bus stop even though I only had twenty bucks left with an empty stomach.

I knew I didn't have enough money for a hotel. I made a bed out of some of my clothes and slept in them. It felt comfortable, and if the morning sun didn't rise and shine through the leaves, then who knew how long I would have stayed outside. I was tired from staying up and not sleeping in the truck. Frank had spent most of the time talking. He'd confessed he often fell asleep at the wheel, which was the reason he was happy to have someone to stop him from dozing off and having a nasty accident.

Morning came way too soon. I stumbled and felt weaker with every step I took. The candy bars in my bag weren't satisfying me. I knew my way home, not because I had any sense of direction, but I was being drawn to it. The smell of the wolves being near told me not to lose hope. I had to perceive and not let my past stop me from getting home.

My instincts were trying to get me to

survive, but as much as I tried to push him out of my head, Winter always flashed into my mind and I hated him for it. Then I would hate myself for hating him even more.

My thoughts became like a hamster on a wheel, going nowhere.

I felt like I walked for hours, dragging my suitcase behind me. One of the little wheels popped off and rolled down the drain. I was about to give up to hitchhike again, when an ambulance blared past onto a street across from me. Wait, that looked familiar. It was the road home.

When I had started this journey, home was the place from which I'd wanted to escape, but I found myself homeless and hungry and so tired I wanted to cry. I wished I had some water and could at least wash my face and make myself presentable, but there was no time for anything as a truck approached me.

It was a red Toyota pick-up truck. Part of me wondered if I dreamed or if it was really my parents' truck. As it drew closer, with the dark shade of red and the black logo of the diner covered the side of the truck. It really was Pa.

He came to a dramatic stop with tires squealing. He wasn't alone. Ma sat next to him in the truck.

With a scowl, he opened the door and I put on a fake smile. I hurried forward and dropped my suitcase. He took it from me and put it to the side on the sidewalk.

"Fagua, my sweet child." He wrapped his arms around me, and he didn't even bother to shut the truck door. He looked as if he'd aged a few years over the last couple of weeks. He had shadows under his eyes.

"We've been looking for you everywhere. We were so worried. We didn't know what to think. We couldn't get a hold of you on the phone."

There was an underlying tense tone to his voice, and it threw me off.

He pulled back, his eyes narrowing. "Did you lose your phone?"

I was about to answer, when he hugged me again.

"It doesn't matter. You're here now. That's all that matters. Here with us again."

Everything happened so fast. Pa wasn't a nervous man, but as he hugged, and kissed me on the cheek. He was scared about something. It had to do with me leaving. He thought he lost me, but I knew better than to think was the only reason.

As for Ma, she just stood by the side of the truck. Pa shoved my case into the back. I moved slowly towards her. She didn't greet me the same way Pa had done. Her blue eyes dulled as I stood beside her.

"Hurry up and get in the truck you two." Pa motioned for me to hop in. Then he climbed in and closed the door.

Tentatively, I reached out and touched her hand. "I'm so sorry, Ma."

"Why the hell did you come back?" she whispered, then yanked open the passenger door.

agua

It was as if I'd never left and the last two weeks in Vegas had never happened. Well, it had been a little over two weeks. Vegas had been the most adventurous thing I'd ever done in my life, everything else had become insignificant.

I'd been back home for two days. I had expected to be grilled, but Pa said I could tell him and Ma what happened in time. Apart from asking why I came back, she hasn't said a word to me.

Every morning she left before breakfast. Pa

said she's hurting and to give her time. Apparently according to him, Ma was so upset when I left, which seemed weird since she asked me why I had come back when she first saw me again. There was nothing sympathetic in her tone, let alone her attitude.

She never asked me how I was feeling or if I was okay. Normal things I'd expect her to say, but she was harsh as if she were disappointed to see me. I wanted us to stop playing this game.

I cleaned the dinner dishes, wishing for the millionth time my folks would invest in a dishwasher like everyone else. Pa read the paper and drank his coffee.

"Um...Pa, I'd like to work in the diner today." I scrubbed at the frying pan coated with a thin, but stubborn, layer of cooked eggs. I wanted the nightmare in Vegas to go away.

"Best check with your Ma, too, but I don't see no reason not to." He cleared his throat, putting aside the paper. "When you disappeared, we told everyone you'd left to visit a sick aunt."

I looked up from the sink. "And they

believed you?" It was only us three. I had no aunts, uncles, or even grandparents.

A scowl hardened his face. "I'm the Alpha, why wouldn't they believe me?"

"Of course. Right." I swallowed and returned to the skillet soaking in sudsy water. Even so, part of me was disappointed about no one caring, but then relieved about not having to answer all the questions about leaving, marrying a human, or the three wolves who had nearly turned my world upside down.

After I finished the dishes, I showered and dressed in my uniform. Ma would be at the diner already, and I didn't want to give her any excuse not to allow me to work again. I had to do something with my time or my mind would torment me about Winter. Did he miss me? Was he okay? And I worried about Sky and if he really was as sick as Husk had acted. I missed them, but not Husk. I was happy to be free from him.

I braided my hair to keep it out of my face and tied the white apron around my waist. My clothes, worn so many years, felt both familiar, yet foreign at the same time.

The walk to the diner took less time than I

remembered. Probably because of my nerves and Ma's attitude toward me since I'd returned. I pushed open the glass door, the bell chimed, and I felt like everyone in the whole place turned and stared at me.

With my head high, I continued straight back to the kitchen when I didn't see Ma anywhere.

"Hey girl," Ted whooped and squeezed me into a giant hug, making my feet leave the floor for a few seconds. "Welcome back."

"Thank you." I laughed, hugging him back.

The burgers on the grill sizzled, and he set me down before flipping the meat over. His thick, black hair was tucked under a hairnet and made him look like a badass rather than our city's wrestling champ. His tats covered his arms, and if I hadn't seen his wolf form, I'd have sworn he was a bear shifter as big as he was. But I thought of him more like the older brother I never had.

"You staying?" He motioned to me with the metal spatula.

"Yup." Didn't want to get into how the longer I was back the more I felt like I was betraying Winter and possibly Sky. I squared my shoulders. They'd lied to me, and I couldn't trust them. "Have you seen Ma?"

"She's cleaning the restrooms."

"Thanks."

He jerked up the basket of fries from the greasier. "Good to have you back, Fagua."

I hurried back to the main area of the diner before I started crying. Like Ted had said, I found Ma scrubbing a toilet.

"What are you doing here?" she asked, not even looking at me.

"I-I want to work, is that okay?"

Instead of answering, she stood and handed me the toilet brush. The bathroom door swung closed. I rolled my shoulders back and bent over the porcelain and cleaned. She hadn't said no or to leave, so I took it as a yes.

Half an hour later, I was about to pour some coffee for ole man Harold, when the glass filled up.

"Fuck!"

I couldn't control myself, it was as if I suddenly was having a vision of an old man Harold being beaten nearly to death. Russ, one of the guys working in the factory, showed no mercy. Harold was trying to escape by trying to change to his wolf form. Every time he tried to shift, he was met with Russ's fists. The crazy part was they were not alone. Not only was Pa there, witnessing it, but other guys from the factory, too.

Harold was our regular, and one of the older members of SmallHeath. Harold did everything on the regular, like come into the diner for his morning coffee. He was a creature of comfort, but this dream I had of him the one with my eyes wide open, I didn't understand or control it. Then it was as if a bolt of lightning had hit me, because I fell to the floor.

Ma rushed to me. "What happened?"

It was the first time she'd spoken to me directly since I'd gotten back. I shook my head as I tried to stand, and she stretched her hand over me.

"Maybe starting work was too soon for you, go to the employee lounge and get some rest or even better go home."

I shook my head. "No, I'll just go out back for a second."

As I stood up, she was already tidying up the mess, and telling everyone to go about their business. Everyone did just as they soon forgot about the breakage and focused on whatever they were doing before I did the mess.

"Ma. Thanks. When Harold comes, would you please give his coffee to him? He doesn't like it cold."

She furrowed her brow, and she said, "Maybe it's better if you go home."

I didn't understand what she was talking about as she drew closer.

"Harold's dead. Fagua, don't you remember?"

I shook my head, wondering if what I'd felt was a dream, or really was the reality. I didn't answer as I rushed to my parents' office and locked the door.

What the hell was going on?

I didn't even know what I was still doing here. Everything felt as if it was all out of control. I could have gone home, but Ma was finally talking to me, and I had questions for her. Like why she clearly didn't want me home, and why she made out she did, when it wasn't the case.

I laid down on the sofa at the corner of the office, and someone jiggled the handle to get in.

"Fuck, the door's locked," someone shouted from the other side of the door.

"We don't need to go in there. Just get rid of the damn body, before Fagua finds out. Just get the shovel from the factory, and I'll wait for you at the back."

"What do I do with the body in the meantime? I don't want it stinking up my trunk."

"We'll leave in the back. I need a fucking smoke, waiting for you to come back."

"Just make sure Afi doesn't see you. He doesn't like smokers. Sign of weakness."

Who was speaking?

I wanted to know who they were on the other side of the door, but I couldn't let them know what I'd just heard, but something was clear, my time here wasn't like before.

Usually, I would go to work in the diner, eat, sleep, catch up on some Netflix and would be it. Now, it was as if I was here with my eyes wide open. I'd completely changed and I couldn't believe in what I'd seen while pouring the coffee. It couldn't have been real, could it? There had to be some reasonable explanation.

Or did I have a real vision? But Ma had said

Harold was dead like it had happened before today.

I had no memory of him being dead. No funeral. No service. Nothing which would make me think he was dead.

As the men's voices faded away, I did one thing. I had to find out what was going on. Who was the person they had at the back of the car? And what did it have to do with me?

I moved to the door, opened it, and no one was here. Luckily, it was the lunch rush, and everyone would be busy out front. This meant going to the back would be easy. I moved to the side like I was in some kind of spy movie.

My heart beat was beating so loud I worried it echoed in the hallway. I took a deep breath and headed to the backdoor. I pushed it slowly, hoping the other guy who was smoking would hide. He was right about one thing, Pa hated smokers. He didn't care about strangers coming and smoking outside the diner. That was fine. He didn't know them, but for people he knew, he preferred to not see them smoke. Sure, he could smell it; he was a wolf after all.

None of what I had overheard made sense. The guys had to have been talking about Pa.

They accepted the rules, not because they respected Pa, but merely because they feared him.

As I made it outside, there was only one car parked outside I didn't recognize. It was a beat-up old Ford. Nearly everyone in town had jeeps or trucks, especially for the rough roads.

I hesitated as I got near the car, then wondered how I would get the trunk open. After looking around to make sure I wasn't spotted, I leaned close to the driver's side door. With my back to it, I tried the handle. It was unlocked. I let out a breath and ducked inside, searching for a key. There wasn't one. But there had to be a lever somewhere. I looked around and found them partially hidden between the driver's seat and window.

Yes!

I pulled the switch to open the trunk, and it popped open. Carefully, I slid out of the car, trying to avoid detection. My breath caught as I made my way to the trunk. Sweat coated the back of my neck.

Inside, there was a body. A man was all bloody and tied up.

I rushed to the side of the diner as my

stomach retched. I vomited into the bushes. Everything I'd eaten this morning rushed out. When I finally finished, I backed away and leaned against the brick wall. I had to find out why those wolves, whoever they were, thought there was some connection with me.

I took a deep breath as I moved back to the trunk, trying to get a better look at the man in the trunk and see if I could identify him. But when I took a step closer to the car, I couldn't move. It was as if I were stuck. I couldn't even open my mouth, but then as I did, I felt a hand over it.

I froze.

Fuck. I'd been caught, but then as I could move, the trunk closed on its own in front of me. There was only one person, I knew who could move things, and it was Ma. Her floral scent filled the air, which she'd worn every day ever since I'd been born, and it had never changed. The body's face turned to show me, who I suspected was in the back. It was the same suit he had worn last time I saw him.

Keith.

One eye was wide open, his dark eye dull, and the other missing. His face was bloody, but

I didn't need to see his face to know it was him. He reeked of death.

I couldn't scream or cry as Ma's hand still covered my mouth. I had nothing left inside me to make me feel sick. No. All I wanted to do was cry. As she slowly removed her hand, she smiled with sadness. Her smile empathized with me, as if to say, I know, I know…

She squeezed her eyes shut briefly and whispered, "I didn't want you to come back. I didn't want you to see what Pa had done."

"Pa," I said, I could hardly speak.

Everything about the past flashed in front of my eyes. Ma wanted to protect me. She needed me to stay as far away from here as possible, or learn the truth. Now, I'd seen what my father had done to Keith and how he never wanted me to leave, I had no intention of ever turning back.

Sky

I felt weak, not the same wolf I once was. It was as if the strength to open my eyes was too much so I just closed them. Even my sense of smell was lost, because before I could tell when both Husk and Winter were in the room. Except the last time I opened my eyes, I could see Winter, and I hadn't even smelled him.

I wasn't just losing my wolf, but I could tell by the sadness in Winter's eyes I was clearly losing my life. I was only thirty years old, but I felt as if I was in my nineties.

Typically, I would have a healthy appetite and want to eat. Now I didn't feel like doing anything.

My mind was trapped in this feeling of all the things I wanted to do and hadn't done. Like I wanted to visit the Grand Canyon, swim with the dolphins in Barbados, which was pretty hard considering I couldn't swim. A sadness crawled inside of me, the feeling of death and not having completed everything I wanted to do in life. The bucket list I should have been checking off instead of trying to find Fagua. We should've enjoyed our lives rather than chasing an elusive dream. We only had one life, and we didn't even appreciate it or live it to the fullest.

In the hallway, Husk and Winter's voices murmured angrily.

No matter what they said, it didn't matter. It was too late.

There was nothing they could do, and one-by-one, we would be dead. This had been the issue. We were acting as if we would never die.

Sure, thirty was too young, but dying would happen one day, whether or not we liked it.

"Shhh," I tried to say it as loud as I could, but it was just a whisper.

"Guys you need to calm down," the doctor said in the hallway. "Whatever you're angry about, you need to keep it outside of this room. Sky has a little time left, and you're making it even shorter by upsetting him. His heartbeat shot up a few seconds ago. I could hear you arguing from my office."

"Winter fucked everything up. Sky could be with us at home. Not here hooked up to the machines ready to die," Husk said in a gruff voice. He was the first of us to get angry, but it wasn't anger I sensed in his voice, it was fear.

"I thought I was doing the right thing. Hoping we would all be good now. I made the wrong choice, and now we'll all pay the price," Winter said in a low voice I had to strain hear.

"Not all of you," the doctor said "Winter you must have mated with her. You're...well you know, healthy," Doc cleared his throat meaning either Husk didn't know or he'd said the wrong thing.

Dizziness pressed me deeper into the

hospital bed and I couldn't hear Husk or Winter. They felt as if they were miles away as if they were in a different world.

I opened my eyes, trying to focus. Then at the corner of the room I made out two figures. Both were dressed in white and seemed to glow inside the hospital. I blinked, wondering if I was having a dream or if this was real. I squinted trying to make out who these two people were when recognition hit me.

"Mom?" I choked out.

She waved, smiling and my dad was beside her. They looked the same age as before when they had their car accident five years ago.

My dad placed his hand on my shoulder. "Son. Don't be afraid."

Mom hugged me. She whimpered and cried. She was so small. It had always been a family joke. She was the tiny one of the family, because she was only five feet, and had such a small frame. Her dark hair hung loose rather than the bun I remember her wearing except on special occasions like a party or time we spent all day at the beach.

I held on to mom with one hand and shifted my head to address dad.

"I'm not afraid. I worry about Husk and Winter. What will they do without me?"

The more I tried to focus to tell them I needed to help my brothers, the more I found myself with them in my arms and us walking together.

Dad was telling me I shouldn't be afraid because he wanted me to follow them. I decided as life was part of life, so was death; I had to embrace it. If it wasn't for now, then it would be in the future.

I took a deep breath and faced mom. "I'm ready to go."

She shook her head with tears in her eyes. "My baby boy. Please, let's see if you have to do this. Let's wait awhile because we may have good news. You may not have to come."

"My love," Dad said, "If he didn't have to come, then he wouldn't be here."

Mom didn't respond to him, she just held on to me tightly, and I did the same. I closed my eyes. It was as if we were in the middle of a white hole. I didn't know where dad wanted to lead me. Mom wanted to wait; she had hope. Something she'd always had.

I remember one time, I'd found a butterfly

in the garden. I told her I wanted it to get better, so she helped me by reading up on how to look after butterflies.

We tended to it, cared for it, until the day it was time for it to heal, and it should have left. It didn't. I told her we didn't do it right. The butterfly didn't fly like we'd read in the book. She said we should give it more time. I'd given up hope, in my eyes the butterfly was dead. Then one day, she told me to come, she lifted the lid, and the butterfly flew out of the box.

Ever since that day, I wished I possessed hope like my mom. I decided unlike when I was a kid, I would follow in her footsteps and seize some as well.

CHAPTER 22

Husk

Back home I paced inside the main suite's living room. "We should be bringing Sky back here with us. Not waiting for the damn doctor and nurses to tell us it was hopeless." I had the stink of illness and death on me, and all I wanted was a shower to scrub myself. But I couldn't relax, not with our brother dying. I couldn't stay here, I'd go back after I cleaned up.

"I know." Winter sank down onto the couch.

He looked miserable, like he hadn't washed his white hair in days. There was a yellow-dullness to it I'd never seen before. But the fact he'd been here and fucked Fagua while I tended our sick brother makes me want to choke him. I snatched a metal vase from the coffee table and hurled it at the patio door. It shattered, making the glass fall like an avalanche.

"This is your fucking fault." I whirled to Winter.

"Mine?" He glared at me. "You're the one who threw the vase."

"Not the fucking vase or the glass." I clenched my fists. "Sky. If it wasn't for your selfishness, Sky would be healed. But no, you wanted Fagua for yourself. You're a little fuck toy."

"Watch your mouth." Winter leapt to his feet. "Don't you ever say that about her again or I'll rip your head off."

I scoffed. "Face the facts, you screwed us over. I bet you didn't even tell her she was our mate—and the cure to our curse."

He didn't have to answer me, his pale face and the quick glance away told me everything.

"What were you going to do, Winter? Keep her for yourself? And I thought I was the bloody bastard of the three of us."

"I made a mistake." He marched to me. "She got under my skin. I-I told her we all had to mate with her and then...then I lost my way. She's an addiction I can't stop," he said the last part under his breath. His blue eyes met mine. "And now she's gone."

"Then go find Keith and drag her ass back here." Why was this so difficult? Both Winter and Sky wanted to pussyfoot around. Fuck no. Lives were at stake. And as much as I didn't give two shits about my own life, Sky deserved better than this. Better than wasting away. He was our youngest brother for fuck sake.

"I can't." Winter pinched the bridge of his nose. "Don't you think I tried? She went back to him—her father and his pack. We've lost her."

"The fuck we have." I growled. "Did she give you the necklace?" The one we'd paid a witch a hell of a lot of money to get and to be able to get Fagua out of there in the first place. Her whole town was under a powerful spell and no outside wolves could get in. Humans, though, could pass in and out without a problem which is why we had grabbed Keith to fetch her and bring her here. Now the whole fucking plan had gone to shit.

"I've no idea. It's not here or the staff or I would've come across it by now."

"If her father gets wind of the magic from the necklace, we're dead."

"We might be dead before that." Winter raked a hand through his hair. "First thing we need to do is get Fagua here so she can fix Sky."

"And how do you think we'll manage that?" I crossed my arms over my chest instead of punching something. Half the time, Winter lived in a damn dream world like Sky. Both of them thought everything would work out perfectly. "Sky beat up Keith for what he did to Fagua and the human ran away. I checked on him two days ago, the nurse said he disappeared."

"He won't tell anyone about us." Winter shrugged and unbuttoned the sleeves on his shirt before rolling them up. "I gave him enough compulsion to think it was a regular job to give Fagua the necklace and bring her here. He doesn't know we're wolves."

"And your power worked so well, he fucking married her." If the bastard were before me now, I'd rip out his balls and shove them down his skinny throat.

"She'll come back." Winter nodded like he tried to convince himself and not just me.

His hope, so much like Sky's, made my heart twist in my chest. Why did I have to be the one with facts and reason? The one who pointed out cracks in reality. The one who watched out and protected them both from the outside world and from themselves?

"You think her father will let her out of his sight again?" I laugh bitterly. "No, he'll have her watched 24/7." It's what I would do. "Hell, he'll probably have the perimeter monitored, too. Even if she wanted to leave and still has the necklace to break through their barrier, she won't have a chance."

And I wasn't going to hold my breath waiting for her either. She'd made it clear last time I'd seen her at our first meal together what she thought of us. As animals and beneath her. We didn't need a mate like that.

Winter squared his shoulders as though preparing for a continued verbal fight. "I have faith she'll come back."

"What? Because you and her bonded and you're cured now?" I barked out a laugh and shook my head. "It doesn't work that way. It's not a one-shot cure all. She has to be mated with you for life, Winter." Well not just him, but he understood my meaning. "You can't fuck her a bunch of times in a few days and expect to be done. If you don't mate with her again before the next moon, you may have bought yourself a little bit of time, but you'll be laying on a hospital bed and fighting for your life just like our brother is right now."

"You don't think I know that?"

"No, I don't. I think you've been thinking too much with your dick."

"Fuck you." He went to the bar in the corner and poured himself a drink before downing it in one gulp. "I look forward to seeing you eat your words when Fagua comes back to us."

"If her father discovers we were the ones who helped get her out in the first place, we won't need a fucking curse to kill us, he'll do it for us."

agua

I backed away from the vehicle with Keith's lifeless, bloodied body in the trunk and shook my head. Ma's words and everything crashed into my head and my heart pounded.

"Hush, Fagua," she cooed and used her magic to shut the trunk before leading me away to the alley on the other side of the diner.

I didn't even realize I was making any noise until she told me. I wiped at the tears falling freely from my eyes. True, I hadn't known

Keith long, but I'd married him. He was my husband and now I was a widow.

"What did they do to him?" I asked, my voice cracking. Even though he'd ran out on me and everything, he didn't deserve death and certainly not in the grisly way it appeared like he'd died.

Ma licked her lips, looking around before answering. "He wouldn't tell your father where you were. He was caught on the road from Vegas. Someone had beaten him up, but paid for his medical treatment. They must have used magic on him because he couldn't remember anything else. Not how to find you or who had hurt him or anything."

"And Pa had him tortured?" Never in a million years would I believe this if I hadn't seen it with my own eyes. I shuddered, wrapping my arms around myself.

"Yes." She swallowed, looking around again. "I tried to protect you from the truth. But when you ran away, I saw I was wrong. You were too believing and trusting so you fled to get out of this town with the first man who came along."

"I tried before...to leave on my own and I never could get past the city limits."

"I know." She tucked my hair behind my ear. "Me and a bunch of other witches set up a barrier. No wolves can enter without our permission, and you can't leave."

Her words felt like a slap to my face. "Why?"

She glanced around hesitantly before letting out a sigh. "You're special, Fagua. And I don't just mean because you're my daughter." She squeezed my hand softly. "You know how our kind are cursed to find their mates before they reach thirty or close to it or they die."

I nodded not sure where she was going with this. Pa was forever going out of town to find mates for our pack members or some-times taking out one or two wolves if their mate wanted to stay living wherever they were.

"You have the potential to have and save more than one mate."

My mouth dropped open as I stared at my conservative mother. The one who wouldn't let me party at all hours of the night or do drugs. I wasn't even allowed to get my ears pierced until I was twenty. I'd begged for years, and she refused. On my birthday, I did it anyway and it was asking for forgiveness instead of permission by the time.

"So Winter was right."

Ma's face paled. "Shhh...don't tell me their names or anything about them. I don't want to know. Knowing can be dangerous for both of us."

A sliver of ice trailed down my spine. "What do you mean?"

"Your Pa isn't who you think he is. What he did to your husband, the human, that's nothing." She swallowed. "I've said too much. You should never have come back here."

"Hey, what are you two doing out here?" Ted marched around the corner.

Ma scrubbed a hand over her face, plastering on a smile before she turned to him. "Just catching up on Fagua's adventures in Vegas. Did she tell you she almost got a wolf tattoo?"

His gaze flicked from her to me. "That so? You're Pa would've flipped his tail and grounded you for a year."

I laughed, but it sounded forced. "What do you think stopped me?"

"I'd have loved to have seen his face though.

Hey," he scratched his rust-colored beard, "People are asking for the special, and we're out of whip cream."

"No problem, I'll go pick some up," I answered.

"Take some money out of the till." Ma gestured toward the diner. "I've got to file some paperwork, and I'll see you when business slows down a bit in the afternoon."

I could tell from her that she wanted to talk to me more, but even though I loved Ted like a brother, it was obvious she didn't want to involve him in our earlier conversation.

An hour and a half later, I wiped down the counter when a honk sounded outside the front of the diner. Two boys playing soccer in the street jogged out of the way of a jeep hurrying through town. The car with Keith's dead body inside was gone. When had they left? I had wanted to find out who was driving and just now noticed the space was empty. A man strolled past with white hair and my breath stuck in my throat.

Winter?

But when he called out to the boys, it was the sunlight making his hair look that color. It wasn't Winter at all.

"Everything okay?" Fiona, one of the other servers, asked. "You look like you're about to rub a hole through the counter there."

"Oh." I stopped wiping and threw the towel in the bucket behind the counter. "Yeah, just some stuck on syrup from breakfast."

Fiona popped a piece of gum in her mouth and clicked her phone on to play one of the addictive puzzle games she liked.

I kept myself busy cleaning up the diner to prepare for the dinner crowd and found my mind drifting constantly back to Winter and Sky. Even to Husk and what he must think of me. No doubt he hated me for leaving, especially if what they said and Ma had told me was real. Sky didn't deserve to die. It wasn't his fault Husk was his brother and an absolute asshole.

And I missed Winter. I closed my eyes for a few seconds, recalling his kiss, his touch and how it felt so good to be in his arms.

By the time the dinner rush was over, I was

about to crawl out of my skin. A desire, a need to go back to the guys nearly overwhelmed me.

If there was a chance—anything I could do to save Sky—then I needed to try. Even though I didn't know him well, he'd been sweet and had made me feel at home with his boyish grin and dark eyes. I owed it to him to do something. But first, I had to figure a way out of here.

I'd wait until midnight tonight, then sneak out and go through a trail I'd traveled countless times when I had wanted to leave before. Something told me this time it would work.

agua

Midnight took forever. I swear, I think all the clocks in the house and on my replacement phone I'd picked up were sabotaging me. Every time I looked, it was only a minute or two later.

I couldn't wait any longer. I grabbed my backpack I'd stuffed with as many clothes and a spare pair of shoes, then tucked my phone into my back pocket. My fingers went to my throat as I tried to remember if I'd forgotten anything. Keith's necklace was cool against my fingertips. I debated yanking it off as I didn't want to remember his mutilated dead body in the trunk. Then my vision blurred until I saw Husk, Winter, and Sky giving the necklace to Keith.

"This is for Fagua. Make sure she wears it or she won't be able to leave the town," Husk said. "We're counting on you to bring her to us."

"Drugging her and kidnapping would be a whole lot easier."

"You lay one finger on her and I'll break your legs." Husk growled.

"Easy," Winter said and both Husk and Keith relaxed, which led me to believe he used his persuasion power. "Just use all the charm you possess and be nice to her."

The scene before me wobbled until I stood alone in my room. I sat down heavily on my bed for a moment. These visions or whatever they were, were coming more frequently. I wanted to ask Ma about them, but she and Pa had gone out dancing, and I had a feeling she'd done so knowing I would try to leave again. This might be my best chance for a long time.

With my mind made up, I stood and crept downstairs. There shouldn't be anyone in the house, but Ma had mentioned me being watched. I couldn't take any chances.

I left all the lights off in the house and slowly opened the backdoor. Before the motion-sensor light flooded the backyard, I quickly unscrewed the bulb. Not so much it would fall out, but enough not to be noticed right away.

Slowly, I made my way down to the fence, and after hefting my backpack over the top, I climbed over.

Crickets chirruped and bullfrogs did their two-tone drone as I hiked down the path past the other homes. I followed the river and swatted away mosquitoes.

My shoe sunk into a muddy hole and I grimaced, trying to get unstuck. This would be a whole lot easier if I could see in the dark as well as wolves. Being a half-breed, my eyesight was only slightly better at night than the average human, but it was pitch-black out here away from town. I was still in the city limits though as we claimed all these woods as ours when SmallHeath was founded.

After I got my shoe out, mud sloshed with every step.

Thunder rumbled in the distance followed by lightning flashing a minute later.

Great.

Fat raindrops pummeled me as I ducked from tree to tree toward the edge of town. The booms between the thunder and lightning streaks grew closer together. I swear the thunderstorm chased me.

Autumn fast approached, and I could tell by the hint of coldness in the air or maybe it was because I was soaking wet. At least it wasn't a blizzard. Which reminded me of Winter. I hadn't even asked how he got his name or his brother's. Lord knows Las Vegas probably never even saw snow. Whereas here in Minnesota, we had ice and snow practically ten months a year.

A howl sounded a few feet from me, and I stilled. My heart pounded in my chest as another wolf answered, then another. How many of them were out here? I crouched behind a cedar tree. Had they seen me?

The rain fell in heavy sheets and helped hide my scent, but I couldn't stay here forever. If they watched the border, then they'd spot me as soon as I made a break for it. If the rain stopped, they'd see me for sure.

And they had the advantage of running on all fours.

I took a steadying breath. Something told me if I didn't do this now, if I didn't try, then I'd never get out of here. Then a deeper feeling hit, like someone had jammed a hook into my stomach and twisted it. I knew without a doubt Sky needed me.

Now.

My adrenaline spiked, and I stood. I could do this. I had to. Winter and Sky counted on me, and I couldn't let them down.

I smirked. Besides, I'd love to see Husk apologize for being such a bully to me. That thought alone gave me the courage to take a step forward, then another.

Five wolves zipped through the clearing with their noses to the ground. Were they already hunting for me? My chest tightened, but I squared my shoulders and continued forward.

A black wolf's ears twitched toward me. It raised its head, snarling low in its chest.

"Let me pass." I held up my hands. "I have to

help a..." I couldn't say mate. Ma had to be wrong about me having more than one. It was only Winter I cared about anyway and who I wanted, but I couldn't let his brother die either if there was any way to save him. "a friend."

The black wolf growled. I didn't recognize him or any of the others.

They surrounded me as they crept closer and closer, tightening the circle.

"Please. I don't want to hurt any of you." I tried to bluff. Though I'd torn apart rooms when Winter and I had sex, I didn't have any control. I had no idea if I could actually make something happen like Ma could whenever I wanted.

A dark figure broke through the bushes wearing a raincoat and boots. He lowered his hood revealing a bald head and mountain man moustache and beard stretched down to his chest. "Where are you going, sweet thing?"

I straightened. "Let me pass. I have important business out of town."

He clicked his tongue, sucking on a tooth. "Shouldn't you be in a car or plane then?"

The wolves didn't back away or even glance back at him.

"Please, just let me go." Maybe I could get back home in time before Ma and Pa returned. In the morning, I could borrow Pa's truck before he awakened and try to drive out of town. I'd have to ditch the vehicle as soon as the sun rose, but it might help me make up for getting sidetracked here.

"Nah." He rubbed his beard. "You are trespassing on our land."

I did a double take. "Your land? This is the forest and part of SmallHeath."

"So?" He crossed his arms, but the wolves around me growled.

I shook my head. "Look, I'm the alpha's daughter. Just let me go. You and your wolves can go back to whatever you like doing out here."

He chuckled. "The alpha's daughter. Are you trying to run away again?"

Shit.

"I told you, I'm on my way to see a friend."

He snorted. "You ain't got no friends outside of our pack."

"Then let me go back home. The alpha will reward you for taking care of me and escorting me." Let them think they'd thwarted my plans. They'd only delayed me.

"We gotta teach you a lesson. You gave your Pa a fright when you left the first time." He lowered his hands and walked toward me. "Spare the rod and spoil the child, I always say. We're gonna teach you a lesson, so you'll never want to try again."

agua

I stumbled backwards as the wolves closed in.

His words promised to deliver exactly what he'd said. I didn't know what he'd do to me, but I didn't like the gleam in his eyes or the wolves around me.

"How come you've never turned, girl? Got too much of your damn Ma in you." He sneered. "All you need is a few bites to get the change fever going. Handy it's a full moon coming up soon."

I'd never been bitten by a wolf my entire

life. "That won't work. If I haven't become a wolf now, I won't ever."

"Only one way to find out. Get her, boys."

The wolf closest to me leapt up, and I screamed, ducking out of the way. Luckily, the wolf missed me and sailed over my head. The man only laughed like he watched the greatest comedy show ever while I experienced a horror movie.

Another wolf charged but stayed low. His fangs dug into my calf. I tripped, falling forward onto my stomach. Pain shot up my leg, and I shook all over. Mud caked all over my body. Another wolf snagged my arm. His teeth pierced my skin. Pain drowned me. I punched him in the nose to get him off me while a third wolf jumped onto my back, but my backpack prevented him from easily reaching the back of my neck.

"Keep biting her," the man yelled. "The half-witch needs more wolf in her in order to change."

He was crazy. No one changed into a were-wolf after being bitten. That was a myth the humans created. And the way these wolves were using me as a chew toy, I was sure they were going to rip me apart.

I had to get them off me. I had to heal Sky and get back to Winter. If I died, the brothers would too if I really was their mate. If I had some ability to heal them from the curse, I couldn't give up. I couldn't die here.

"No," the word came out a whisper.

The wolf biting my forearm let go, but his low menacing growl told me he was going to bite me again. I kicked the wolf on my leg off and pushed up as hard and fast as I could.

I threw my hands out. "Stop."

But none of them listened. They circled me with the man cheering them on.

"You know what? We smell another wolf on you." He smirked. "One not of our pack. Your daddy was real mad about you running off and marrying a human. What do you think he's gonna do with this news? You fucked a wolf he hasn't sanctioned. Tell us who he is and where to find him, and the pain will stop."

He had to be the one who'd driven the car with Keith's body in the trunk. Bile burned the back of my throat at the thought.

Instead of answering, I shook my head.

"Stubborn, eh? Well, I know just the cure for that." He unhooked his belt and unzipped his pants. "Let me fix that for you."

A million emotions slammed into me, all wrapped in terror and disgust.

He reached down for me, but I threw my hands out with a scream. A blast of wind smacked into him and all the wolves around me, knocking them back into the trees.

Had I done that?

I didn't wait around to find out. I pushed to my feet and started to run, which ended up being more like limping hops with my leg bleeding and pain radiating from the bite. This had to be a nightmare. I'd wake up back in Winter's bed with his arms around me. I'd tell him all about this horrible dream, and he'd tell me I was safe. Then he'd kiss me, and we'd make love.

Every step, I kept in the forefront of my mind.

I chanted his name in my mind over and over again.

At the road, I let out a breath, but the wolves howled behind me, giving chase.

Why hadn't I thought this through? Had a

car waiting for me or mapped out the quickest way to the next town so I could ride the bus? Now I was injured, bleeding, and my vision was tunneling like I was going to pass out.

I had to focus. If I fainted, they'd find me and haul me back to my father. And I didn't trust these wolves not to rape me or worse. My magic had blown them away. Though, I didn't think I could do it again, not as weak as I felt.

A car whizzed past so fast I swore they were going fifty miles over the speed limit.

"Hey," I yelled, waving my good arm and shuffling forward. But taillights vanished into the darkness.

Another car puttered past and when I put my thumb out to hitchhike, they moved into the other lane to go around me. My legs buckled, and I fell onto my knees. The asphalt dug into my skin.

My hands shaking, I crawled forward, trying to put as much distance between me and my attackers.

"There she is," the man yelled. The wolves howled and snarled.

A police siren sounded, but it was too late. I

would be dragged back into the woods. I couldn't let that happen. I couldn't.

Car lights flashed around the curve, but I couldn't even lift my head or cry out. Everything around me faded to darkness.

~

Sky

A cry sounded behind me. I let go of my father and mother's hand and glanced over to find Fagua laying halfway across a road with a car speeding toward her.

"Sky?" my mom asked, her ethereal form fading. "What are you doing?"

But there wasn't time. If I didn't do something, Fagua would die. I ran forward along a misty cloud until I was running so fast, I flew. Just like before, I sailed through the air. Except, I was faster than anything, faster than a jet. The car swerved and avoided hitting Fagua by an inch. Relief swept through me, but then a man with five wolves burst onto the scene. I didn't like how he smiled at Fagua.

"Bring her back boys. No one gets away from me."

Hatred boiled in my veins. I rushed forward to fight him, but I sailed right through him.

I looked down and my hands were see-through. No! I couldn't help her if I was a damn ghost. I had to save her, even if it meant staying dead. A buzzing sound filled my ears. I stepped between Fagua and the approaching wolves.

The animals whimpered, backing away from me.

"What's wrong with you fuckers?" the man bellowed. "Come here."

But they whined, backing away and not taking their eyes off me. The car spun around, turning their high beams on and blinding the man.

"Fagua," I yelled, but she lay motionless on the road.

A tingling burrowed into my chest, and I winced. I couldn't give into the sensation or the fading voice of my parents calling me. Fagua was in trouble. I had to help her. Had to at least keep the wolves away, and they seemed to sense I was here. The big guy would be the problem though.

He chuckled, shaking his head at the whining wolves. "If you want anything right, you gotta do it yourself. I'm going to teach this bitch a lesson."

I memorized his bald head and scraggly moustache and beard. He'd tried to hurt my mate. I raised my fists to pound his face, but he went right through me like I wasn't even there. Fagua lay motionless on the road, and he headed straight for her.

My spirit body was fading. A strong tug yanked my middle. I couldn't stay.

"No!" I yelled. "Fagua!"

Blackness swirled around me. I couldn't move as it swallowed me whole.

Winter

Sky's heart monitor blared an alarm, and I jumped. His breathing had stopped.

"What's happening to him?" I rushed to his hospital bed.

"I don't know." Doc placed grabbed the defibrillator pads and amped up the power. He placed them on Sky's chest. "Clear." The machine buzzed. Electricity arched through my brother's body, and his back bowed.

The machine showed a straight line on the screen.

"Again."

My stomach clenched as I watched the doctor and nurses try to bring my brother back. This was all my fault. I had known Sky was sick, but not this badly. After I'd gotten the first message from Husk about he and our brother hanging out in town, I didn't question. I was too busy enjoying my time with Fagua and had never checked my phone again until she disappeared.

Now my brother is dead because of it.

I leaned against the wall, feeling like I was going to be sick while they used the paddles two more times.

A faint beep made the breath lodged in my chest loosen. Another beep sounded.

"He's all right?" I pushed forward, having to see for myself.

But Sky lay pale on the hospital bed hooked up to more wires. His chest rose and fell shallowly with the aid of a breathing tube.

"He's stable, for now." Doc handed the paddles to a nurse who cleaned them and hooked them back onto the machine. "I'm afraid he's not going to be with us much longer."

"What do you mean?" I didn't want to know. I wanted to turn back time and correct my mistakes, fix everything I'd done wrong. It should be me or Husk in Sky's place, not our youngest brother fighting for his life.

"Sky has slipped into a coma. The machines are breathing for him, but I don't know if he'll wake up." Doc squeezed my shoulder. "I wish I had better news. Once this happens, I haven't seen a wolf come back from the space between the living and the dead."

I nodded, unable to speak, and sank down into the visitor chair next to Sky's bed. What was I going to do? I couldn't lose Sky. And Husk was out picking up cards and shit to keep Sky busy while he was here in the hospital. Now he was going to find out our brother might never open his eyes again. Might never tell us to fuck off.

It had been days since Fagua had disappeared, and with each passing hour, the hope I'd had of her returning withered. Now Sky was in a coma. What could she possibly do in order to heal him? She and I had made love, which had healed me. But she couldn't even kiss Sky except on his cheek or forehead with him unconscious and a damn breathing tube down his throat.

I placed my face in my hands, feeling like I couldn't breathe. My selfishness might cost my brother his life. I'd had plenty of time to bring Fagua to him. Yet, I kept stalling, telling myself one more hour with her, one more day, one more night.

Pulling my hands away from my face, I leaned back in the chair. I deserved to be in this hospital bed, not Sky. Out of the three of us, he was the best, not bitter like Husk and not unemotional like me. Usually, I could keep my heart and mind separate to do what needed to be done. All I wanted to do was see my brother grin and allow him to be wild and free as he raced through the woods. Hell, I'd even take him flying through the air. It used to scare the crap out of me, thinking someone would see him.

Now, he'd never be able to shift into his wolf. We'd never hunt together or try out his new jokes to see if we could get Husk to crack a smile.

Husk entered the room and stopped in the

doorway. "Sky," his voice sounded hoarse. "What the fuck happened?"

"He stopped breathing. Doc has him on machines to keep him ali—"

"Don't you fucking say it." He growled, but tears glistened in his eyes. "Don't. He'll recover. He'll be fine."

I stood unable to watch both my brothers be ripped apart. One from a curse, and the other from not being able to do a fucking thing to stop it.

Out in the hallway, Doc talked in hush voices with two nurses. When he saw me, he waved me over and the nurses left.

"I want you to know we're doing everything we can for Sky. But the best thing we can do is make him comfortable."

"How long?" I swallowed and my throat felt like I'd filled it with pieces of glass and sand. "How long does he have?"

"Two days at the most." He winced. "Any news from his mate?"

I shook my head, no longer believing in miracles.

Fagua

Tires squealed and I winced as a major migraine pounded in my temples like a herd of marching elephants. I could've sworn that Sky was here. I thought I'd heard him call my name, but that wasn't possible, was it?

"Get her, hurry up," a familiar voice sounded.

"Touch her and you're dead," the man from the forest yelled.

"Don't listen to him. Hurry, Ben."

I knew that voice. Rebecca, my best friend. But when I tried to open my eyes, I felt like they were swollen shut, and the elephants started a larger stampede across my skull.

Strong hands lifted me, and I caught the whiff of peppermint and tobacco underneath.

A thunk sounded behind us.

"Damn witch!" A male voice snarled.

The wolves howled and yipped while whoever carried me hurried forward. I was thrown into the back of a jeep, and then the vehicle sped down the road.

"Oh my god, Fagua, are you okay?" Rebecca

asked, reaching over the passenger seat to touch my shoulder. "What did those bastards do to you?"

Were they taking me back home? I couldn't. Pa would handcuff me to his side if I did. I'd never get another chance to escape after this…Ever. "Stop, let me go."

"What? No way." Rebecca snorted.

"No, I can't," I licked my lips that felt dry and cracked along with the metallic taste of blood. "I have to go to Las Vegas."

"Shit." Ben's voice was low and tense. "This is fucked up, Rebecca."

"I know, I know." She turned in her seat and handed me a bottle of water. "Here."

I didn't think I could even lift my head, but I tried anyway. I sipped the water until my headache eased enough where I could open my eyes. "Thank you. Just drop me off at the nearest bus station, and I'll be out of your hair."

Though when I felt around, my backpack was gone along with my wallet and cellphone. Shit!

Rebecca's look said no way in hell. "You know I have a sixth sense about things."

I nodded, but stopped fast when the pain returned to my head and really all over.

"Well, ever since you got back, you've had a dark cloud over you." She gave a sideways glance at Ben. "You found them, didn't you? Your mates?"

"Well fuck, does everyone in the whole universe know, but me?"

She laughed. "I don't envy you girl. One man is plenty enough for me to handle."

My flush heated my entire face. "Um...thank you for helping me, but you'll both be punished. Pa will—" the image of Keith's dead body stuffed into a trunk flashed before me.

"We know." Rebecca gave me a watery smile. "Actually, we don't plan on going back, ever. Your Pa isn't a good alpha or wolf, Fagua. He'll punish us for leaving and for interfering and helping you get away." She wiped away tears. "I'm so sorry I didn't try to tell you sooner about what kind of wolf your father is, but he would've had us killed."

"It's okay." I reached over and hugged her from the backseat. "I never wanted to listen and I know I stopped you from telling me several times."

"Still, I wish I had done more."

I nodded, my world feeling like it was upside down and inside out. I told her everything that had happened to me and about how I was still coming to terms with having three mates and about how my magic went haywire when I had sex with Winter, but not with Keith.

"Three?" Her blond eyebrows rose into her bangs. "Wow. No wonder whenever I tried to find out who your potential mate was I got dizzy."

"I'll fill you in more on the way." Something inside me said if we didn't travel fast, I would be too late. "Please. I-I need to get to Las Vegas as soon as possible."

"We can't take the train or planes. He'll have men watching." Ben nodded, pulling onto the freeway.

Rebecca squeezed my hand. "We'll drive straight through, each of us taking turns without stopping except for gas and such."

"D-Do you see me making it in time?" I had to ask, even though my heart clenched at the thought of her answer. Sky had helped me back there with the wolves. I was sure of it.

"I-I don't know. There's a darkness tied to you that might be one of your mates." She blinked hard. "I'm sorry, Fagua...we might be too late."

CHAPTER 27

Husk

My knuckles bled and were sore from punching the brick wall outside the hospital. And I still didn't fucking feel any better. Upstairs, Sky was hooked up to more machines than I'd ever seen in one room before. He was fighting for his life while I walked around and doing whatever I wanted.

And Winter... I clenched my fists, fighting the urge to return outside and punch the bricks again. Well, he'd screwed our brother over for her, a flighty woman who'd fled at the first fucking chance she got. She wasn't my mate, no matter what Winter or Sky or anyone else bloody thought. My mate wouldn't have left; she'd have fought.

Sky was in a coma and Doc didn't think he'll come out of it. I didn't get to tell him goodbye. Or that he'd made me proud to be his older brother. Tears burned the back of my fucking eyes and I grumbled as the elevator took too damn long to open.

This morning Doc planned taking Sky off life support. Said he'd been on it too long and we're just prolonging his pain. Doc and Winter's words, not mine. I won't ever give up on my brother. Never. I wanted to tell him to get his ass out of bed. That the sky is full of white fluffy clouds, just like he loved when he flew. They helped hide him from the humans who'd freak out if they saw him.

A bitter laugh escaped my aching chest. Damn Sky for taking the curse first. Hell, it should've been me. I was the eldest with Winter always trying to play peacemaker as the middle brother. And Doc said we gotta pull the plug today. I'd been outvoted by Winter, Doc, and Sky's stupid living will.

I pushed open the hospital door to find

Fagua looming over Sky with Winter on the other side of the bed from her.

"What the fuck is going on here," I bellowed. "Get her the fuck away from him."

"Nice to see you too, Husk." She glanced over her shoulder at me.

Her eyes had dark circles under them as if she hadn't slept in several days. What did she want, a medal for finally feeling guilty that she'd fled when she could've prevented this? Or at least given a fuck to try.

"I mean it." I shoved deeper into the hospital room. Winter leapt to block my path. "Get her out of here. I don't want her near Sky. She'd done enough."

"Let her try." Winter coaxed, but even his damn talent of persuasion can't get through my rage.

"No." The words emerged almost as a hiss.

Fagua's shoulders sagged. "Look, I made a mistake. Let me try to fix this."

"She's right, Husk," Doc said from the doorway. "This is his only chance, and it might be too late."

I shook my head to rid myself of what he'd said. It felt like an execution sentence. "How the fuck is she going to do anything?" I waved a hand at her. "She can barely stand up."

For all we knew, she could have been working for that bastard father of hers and was here as a spy or led him right to us.

Doc cleared his throat. "I've already pulled all the machines off him."

"What?" I roared, but Winter grabbed me before I could tear into the doctor.

"I told him to do it while you were outside. Five minutes later, Fagua came."

With a shove, I pushed Winter off me. They didn't know shit. Our brother was dying, and it was all her fault.

"Okay, what do I need to do to help him?" Fagua asked, the hope in her eyes nearly undoing my resolve to hate her.

"What did you do that fixed Winter?" Doc pointed his chin at my brother.

Fagua turned a deep shade of purple. "I-I don't think that's possible in Sky's condition right now."

"Well, think of something fast. His heart rate and blood pressure are dropping."

She straightened and turned back to Sky. "I know you came and saved me the other night. Made those wolves scared to come after me and bought me time. Thank you."

I scoffed. Winter shushed me and glared until I stomped over to a corner and crossed my arms as I leaned against the wall.

"If it wasn't for you, I don't know where I would be right now." She brushed his caramel-colored hair out of his face. "Wherever you are, I wish I had more time to get to know you. I wasted so much being strong-willed and stubborn."

"That's putting it mildly."

"One more word, Husk," Fagua said without looking at me, "And I'll have you thrown out of here."

Winter held back a grin. I fought the urge to punch him.

"Please come back to us, Sky." She took his hand in hers. "I know you can hear me. Together we can figure this out, I promise. But I can't do it without you. I want you to teach me how to fly. I want to feel the joy you bring to the world." She bent over him, kissing his temple, then brushing her lips across his slowly.

She whispered something in his ear that even with my wolf senses, I couldn't discern.

Then she leaned back, still holding his hand. "I'm not leaving Sky. I'll wait here all day if I have to. Please don't give up on us when we haven't even started."

I arched an eyebrow at Winter. So now she believed she was our mate? Or was this all a ruse to convince Sky to fight to live?

Tears fell down her face. "Please Sky. Forgive me. I want to make this right."

My wolf hearing picked up the sound of his heartbeat as it skipped, and it felt like a vice clamped down on my chest.

"No," Fagua cried, sinking down beside the bed. "I can sense him and he's drifting further away."

I wanted to run forward and shake him. Tell my brother to stop playing around and get the fuck back here. But my legs felt like they wouldn't support me. I did it anyway. I walked one step at a time until I reached the end of his bed. I placed my hands on his feet.

"Damn you, Sky, get your ass back in your body."

Winter choked out a cry, but then he

nodded and went to Sky's left, opposite of Fagua. "Yes, Sky, come back to us." The pull of his magic was so strong, I swore my soul wanted to do his bidding, too.

She laid her forehead down on Sky's, breathing in deeply. Then Fagua kept one hand on Sky's, before placed the other on his chest and kissing him on the mouth. Her body shuddered, and she stumbled, but kept her position.

I wanted to ask Winter what the fuck was happening, but the lights in the room flickered.

Hundreds of questions banged around in my head. They'd all have to wait because I felt like I was being drained dry. I glanced over to Winter. He was on his knees, sweat glistening on his forehead and his brow pinched. Even Fagua appeared a little green as she half-laid on Sky and the bed like she was holding on to keep from falling on the floor.

My own knees buckled, and I went down hard, but I kept contact with Sky.

His heart rate jumped again. It wasn't working. Whatever the hell Fagua was doing was killing us right along with Sky.

CHAPTER 28

agua

I felt like my soul was being ripped from me piece by piece. And I didn't know if I'd gotten rabies from the damn wolf bites because I'd only had time to dose with peroxide on my mad dash here or if it was something worse.

All my insides felt like they were on fire and someone had thrown gasoline on them.

I wanted to scream, but I couldn't. I was frozen in place. Frozen in this never-ending nightmare as my life was being leached out of me. My whole body shook, and I couldn't pull away. God, I thought I was dying right along with Sky. And I felt Winter and Husk's presence with me. Were they being affected too? I didn't have the strength to lift my head or even open my eyes to find out. I trembled as wave after wave of searing pain drowned me.

A cool wind blew against my face, and I felt Sky's playfulness dancing in the room.

He took a huge breath and whatever power holding me snapped like a rubber band. "Wow, now that was a fucking wild ride."

"Sky," I choked, tears streaming down my face. His essence mingled with mine, and it was more intimate than if we'd had sex for days straight.

"Hi," he said weakly, but color already returned to his cheeks.

He reached a hand to my cheek and cupped my face. I leaned into his touch. I'd done it. I'd healed him even though I had no clue how.

"Sky?" Winter reached down and hugged him. "We thought you were gone."

"I was," he said. "I was with our folks and flying fast and far from here. But then I heard you all talking to me. I couldn't understand the words. I only got the feeling if that makes any sense."

"No, it doesn't make any fucking sense. It's stupid witchcraft nonsense." Husk pushed from the floor with a scowl. He wobbled on his feet and sat down on the corner of Sky's bed.

"How did you heal him when you two didn't have sex?" Winter asked.

"It's different for everyone," a doctor wearing a white coat and glasses came into the room. "If only one thing worked between mates to cure them, then everyone would do it, and we wouldn't have this curse hovering on top of us, would we?"

"May I have a moment alone with Sky?" I asked. Winter pulled a chair out for me.

Husk glared, but the doctor and Winter left.

"So is this where you cure me with sex?" Sky tucked the pillow higher behind his head. "Cause I gotta say that would be awesome compared to getting poked and prodded."

. . .

I laughed, but my face heated at the thought. Ma's words about me having more than one mate repeated in my mind. Not to mention I'd had plenty of time on the road to get tips from Rebecca on how to control my magic whenever I had sex. "Were you out on the road a few nights ago?"

"Yes. I don't know how I got there." He frowned. "One moment I was with my parents and ready to join them. But then something inside me screamed you were in trouble and needed me. Then I flew toward you. But not like when I could in my physical form. I zipped to you faster than a rocket."

I nodded for him to continue.

. . .

"I saw and heard you. Even smelled you and felt you." He reached out his hand to me and I took it. "I wanted so bad to tell you it was going to be okay. That I was here for you, but you couldn't hear me. Only the wolves could."

His hand felt cool in mine. My throat tightened at the thought I might have made it here too late, and we wouldn't have been having this conversation. "I sensed you, if that makes sense. I knew it was you who kept the wolves away from me and bought me time."

"I wish I could've done more. And I still need to pay that bastard a visit." He sat up, then winced, his breath turning to pants.

.   .   .

"Don't worry about him. I'm safe now." From what Ma had told me, I didn't want Sky or Winter or even Husk anywhere near my Pa. Look what his men had done to Keith, and he wasn't even a wolf or from a rival pack.

"So you're staying...with us?" There was so much hope in his voice it made my heart hurt. His eyes brightened.

"Yes. I'd like to." I bit my lip, not sure if Husk was onboard or not. I hadn't talked to Winter since I left. Would he even want me back after I left him without talking to him or leaving a note while his brother was on death's door?

CHAPTER 29

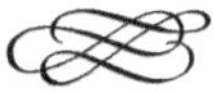

Sky

"It is so good to be home," I stretched out on the pool float with a beer in one hand and my shades in place.

"Don't let it go to your head," Winter chided from the patio door. "It's your turn to do all the dishes after dinner."

I waved him off as Fagua slid into the pool wearing a red bikini. I tried not to stare at her. She and Winter had made up. Listening to them have sex last night was nearly too much for me. Husk had stormed out being his usual stubborn self and hadn't returned all day. He'd probably slink back in when dinner was ready in an hour or so.

"By the way," I said, lowering my sunglasses as she swam over to me, "I don't think I ever thanked you for healing me. Without you, I would've died."

"I was happy to help. And you saved me, too. I'd still be stuck at home with my Pa if not for you." She tilted her head to the side and gave me a teasing smile. "So when do you think your powers will come back?"

"Not sure." I was still weaker than I'd liked from my hospital stay. "Why, you want me to take you flying up in the clouds?"

She ran a hand along the bright green pool float. "Maybe. It would be handy to check on my friend Rebecca. Her and her husband helped me that night, too. We drove all day and all night to get here in time."

"Where are they now?"

"California. They were running from my Pa, too." She swallowed. "They can't ever go back home."

"Are you upset you can't either?" I brushed my fingers across her cheek.

"I thought I would be, you know. But it's not like I remember it." She looked out to the horizon, deep in thought. "The first time I left it was because I was bored and wanted a change. I was sick of being stuck in our town, never going anywhere, and had just clicked with Keith. Or so I'd thought."

I tapped a finger on her necklace. "We paid a lot of money to get this to you. No way you'd been able to break through the town's magical protection without it."

"My Ma and the other witches did that. I think they tied me to the town so I could never leave." She shuddered. "I never realized what a monster my dad was. When I saw Keith's dead body stuffed in a trunk, I still can't believe it."

It was so much worse, but I couldn't tell her everything we knew. She'd suffered so much and still healed from those fucking werewolves who had bitten her. And I was glad Keith was dead and glad it had nothing to do with me or my brothers. Didn't want that on my conscience. But beating the snot out of those who hurt her and tried to keep her from me...from us, yeah, they were going to get paid back in full.

"I will protect you."

"No," she said, looking too damn sexy all

wet and in her skimpy bikini. "We'll protect each other."

~

With our toes and fingers wrinkled, Sky and I darted out of the pool to get dry and ready to eat. I wrapped the towel around my wet body. Sky stared at me like I was a big juicy lollipop he wanted to lick all over. Just the thought made my insides tighten in anticipation.

"May I kiss you?" he asked quietly, as if afraid he'd offend me.

I thought he'd never ask!

"Of course, Sky." I stepped closer and put my hands on his waist. "I thought you'd never ask."

He pulled me to him instantly, eagerly, and tilted my face up to his. Our lips brushed together softly at first, once, twice, then on the third kiss, he pressed his lips to mine harder, with more passion. A pleasing grumbling sound came from deep in his throat, and I groaned back. It felt so good to have him kiss me.

Sky stepped forward, then continued until I came up against the wall. He kissed me in the darkness of the hallway until his tongue brushed against my bottom lip.

I opened my mouth, eager to take this further. His kiss was both hungry and demanding. I followed his lead and twirled my tongue around his. When he sucked at my tongue, my knees nearly buckled. We kissed until our bodies strained toward each other.

"Let's go inside," he said, almost breathless when he pulled away.

"Aren't we already inside?"

He chuckled, nipping at my lower lip playfully. "I meant inside one of the bedrooms."

"How about mine?"

"Works for me. Unless you want to do this on the roof?"

I inhaled sharply "Next time." If we went upstairs, he'd probably fly me around. I didn't want to stop kissing or touching him.

His hands cupped my face, and his lips came back down to mine. He pulled me closer until my aching breasts pressed into his chest.

I wanted him naked. Wanted him inside me now with a hunger I couldn't fathom. We kissed all the way to my room.

Inside, I didn't even bother closing the door, but placed my hands on both sides of his face as he turned to lean against the wall.

I wasn't averse to taking the dominant stance and wiggled at the thrill surging through my body. My hard nipples against his bare chest thanks to my thin bikini. The chandelier in the hallway tinkled loudly, and I inhaled a deep breath, calming the center of me where my magic lay. I had told Rebecca about Winter and how my magic went haywire whenever I had sex with him. She had said it was because he was my mate—or one of them. Her jaw had dropped when I told her how Winter and his brothers said I was the mate for all three of them. So far, Rebecca's suggestions on how to keep my magic from rampaging whenever I got turned on or had sex worked.

My attention flashed back to Sky. He was taller, so when I laid my hands against the wall to either side of his head my breasts pressed more tightly into his chest. He groaned as he teased my lips with his. His hands wrapped around my waist, and he hauled me tight against his cock.

He was so damn hard big like Winter. The thought sent a shudder of desire through me. Sky shifted against the wall, spreading his legs to bring me firmly between his muscular thighs.

I was eagerly ready to explore all of him in all kinds of positions.

No thoughts of anything else except right here and now with Sky and his heat filling my senses as our mouths tangled and I held on to him. His hands dug into my hair, holding me in place. My hands skimmed down his chest and over his hard muscles.

He pulled back to look down at me with bedroom blue eyes shining like diamonds in the moonlight.

"You sure about this, Fagua?" Sky's voice trembled slightly as though his excitement was causing him to lose control.

"I want to fuck you, Fagua. And I don't just mean right here, right now. I mean forever. Are you sure that's what you want?"

"Yes." I'd never wanted anything more in my life. Well, except when I had sex with

Winter. No other man except him made me feel this way. This desperation was like I was going to go crazy and explode if I didn't have him.

"I want you, Sky. And as crazy as it might sound to anyone else, I want this. I want you. Please, don't stop," I murmured against his neck, eager to make him see he didn't need to pause on my account. Sky leaned his head back so I could bite at his neck more. We weren't vampires, but something about this vulnerability and grazing skin made me even hornier.

I nibbled at his skin, tasting his cologne and his own uniqueness. The guttural sounds he made each time had me soaking my bikini bottoms. I sucked at each spot I bit with gentleness.

"What about your brothers?" I asked, feeling a little awkward about it. I mean, yeah, they'd talked about me being their mate and all, but would Winter really be okay with this? With me having sex with Sky? And I was sure Husk would hate it as he always left the suite whenever I was intimate with Winter.

"No, they don't care."

I wasn't so sure about that and hesitated.

"If you want me to stop, say the word."

"Kiss me again," I said.

I lost myself in his kiss and it wasn't long before he carried me to the bed. I wrapped my legs around his waist, never breaking our kiss. He sat on the bed, holding me, and I pushed him down until he laid on his back. I straddled him as I removed my top. I needed to feel his hands on me, to feel his mouth everywhere. I unhooked my bikini top and flung it out of the way.

I hungered to feel his naked skin against mine. Wanted to taste every inch on him from the

silky-smooth expanse of his chest, to his chiseled abs, and all the way down if he'd let me. I yearned to explore him.

"You're making me feel like I'm a horny teenager again" He cupped my breasts, rubbing his thumb across the nipples.

I gasped out a breath. "Me too. I want you." I ran my index finger down his muscular chest.

My hand drifted lower before I teasingly brought it back up. I touched his bottom lip and slowly traced my finger over it, before I replaced my finger with a kiss.

I moved lower, tasting his deliciousness as I went. First down his neck, then along his collar bone. I took my time to memorize every part of him. My nipples slid down his body and my breasts felt huge against his chest.

I grazed over his flat abs and down to the line of his groin. I held my breath and pulled the trunks down. Forget foreplay, I was hungry and needed him so bad I was desperate for release. I tucked my hand inside his trunks and pulled his cock free.

We both wore slightly damp swimwear stuck to our bodies like glue, but I managed to free him. He was already hard and erect and perfect like the rest of him.

I slid my hand along his silken flesh. He groaned with each stroke, making me feel powerful. Liquid heat coiled low in my belly. I wanted more and lowered my mouth to his thick length, tasting him with a flick of my tongue.

"Fagua," he nearly shouted my name and thrust into my mouth. The feeling was so sensual as he hit the back of my throat before nearly pulling free, then plunging back inside.

He moved beneath me, slow and certain of

how he wanted it, taking some of my control, but I enjoyed the give-and-take.

Need consumed me, my pussy dripping wet and pulsing for his touch.

His sounds of pleasure, along with my body's reactions made me want him to come in my mouth.

"Fuck, I want to fuck you," Sky said. His cock throbbed in my mouth. He gently pulled me to him and kissed me breathless.

Then he rolled me over, yanking down my bikini bottoms in one swift movement. I giggled, but his intense look made me self-conscious about my reaction.

"I've wanted to kiss you since the moment I met you and you threw your purse on the bed and demanded we leave your hotel room. You are so beautiful and brave. I dreamed of you just like this, beneath me, wet for me, so ready for me," he whispered, kissing all the way down my hip bones.

My breath hitched as his lips gently slid over my bare pussy. His fingers parted my glistening lips. He lowered his mouth over me, his tongue flicking in and out until I lost any ability to think. I cried out in pleasure as Sky sucked on my clit.

My climax built while I bucked against his mouth.

His tongue stroked from the very edge of my pussy and then up to circle at my clit, licking it, sucking it until shivers of pleasure shot through my stomach and straight into my brain. I gasped loudly while my hips pressed down into his face.

"Don't stop, Sky. Please fucking don't stop." I said as his tongue moved on me, driving me higher, until I wasn't sure if we were flying.

His tongue flicked at my clit mercilessly. An aching pleasure spread until it became difficult to breathe, and I was moaning and panting.

I looked down at his head between my thighs. His mouth moved over me. Involuntarily, my thighs clamped around his head. My body convulsed with a pleasure.

"Sky." I groaned his name. My back bowed and all my muscles tightened before releasing like they'd turned into jelly.

Cries of my pleasure echoed around me, and the tingling sensations washed over me. I was lost to the overwhelming bliss. And before one climax ebbed, a new one arose hard and fast.

Sky leaned back, a sexy, satisfied look on his face.

I felt nearly boneless from the euphoric state I found myself in.

He settled between my thighs and pushed me a little further up the bed and wrapped my legs around his hips.

"Please," I tried to ground down on him, my libido surging again.

He thrust into me swiftly, filling me completely. "God, you're so wet."

I mewled as he pumped into me. "You feel so good."

He slid out of me slowly, his gaze taking me in and making me even wetter.

"Fucking beautiful," he whispered, then growled. "I knew you'd have a tight pussy, but it is super tight."

He tucked my legs over his shoulders as he knelt below me. The new position made it feel like his cock was even bigger, and I dug my fingers into the mattress as another orgasm roared closer.

"Fuck, you're going to make me come." He

thrust into me, but I couldn't answer as gasps of pleasure broke through my lips.

I lifted partially, grasping his arms as he leaned forward with my legs pressed over his shoulders. My pussy pulsed around him, making me feel so good I never wanted to stop.

Sky ran a finger over my lips, not stopping his thrusting. "I can't wait to fill your mouth, Fagua. Your full lips and—fuck." He pulsed harder and faster. I sucked on his thumb and his thrusts sped up.

"I can keep her mouth occupied," Winter said from the doorway, stroking himself.

He was completely naked, and I practically drooled. Two at once? Never had that, but my pussy clenched around Sky's cock in anticipation.

"Come and join us, if that's all right with you, Fagua?" Sky asked, pulling his thumb from my mouth.

"Yes," I breathed out.

Winter didn't wait, but joined us on the bed. I turned my head to face him and licked the precum off the tip of his cock. Winter groaned, sliding past my lips and into my mouth. While he slowly moved deeper into me, Sky thrust in and out of me and my pussy grew wetter, making me quiver with each thrust.

Winter grasped the back of my head, guiding me down further onto his cock. I moaned as wave after wave of pleasure crashed into me. My muscles went rigid at the start of my release, and as if on cue, both guys drove into me, bringing me over the edge until a tidal wave of ecstasy had me sailing into the stars.

"Fuck, fuck, fuck," Sky groaned as his pace increased.

My breasts bounced with each thrust. Winter's fingers flicked my nipple, and I screamed around his cock as another orgasm ripped through me.

Sky stilled, his cock buried deep inside me as his pleasure softened his face. He leaned forward, kissing my breast before pulling out. Yet he continued to stroke my folds as Winter pushed all the way into the back of my throat. Sweat dotted along his forehead.

"I'm going to come," Winter said, holding the back of my head.

I moaned, letting him glide me up and down on his cock as my answer. Needing no further encouragement, his fingers lightly dug into the back of my scalp as he thrust. It was so sensual and raw that my body trembled with another orgasm.

His hot seed burst into my mouth, and I swallowed over and over again.

Sated, he eased from between my lips and gave me a sexy smile that sent my heart going pitter-patter.

Sky hauled me further onto my bed and pulled me into his arms. My back pressed against his chest as he nuzzled the back of my neck. I was sweaty and spent, but so satisfied I didn't think I'd be able to move again. Winter shifted into bed with us with him facing me.

"You can hardly keep your eyes open, Fagua, sleep." He kissed my mouth lightly. "Tomorrow we can do this all over again. Though I get dibs on your sweet pussy."

Sky yawned. "I'll take your mouth or ass, doesn't matter to me as long as I get to make you come."

I settled into their embraces, content and happy for the first time in my life.

What would it be like to have pleasure like this not just tonight, but every day of the week by these two handsome men?

My mates. What about three men fucking me at the same time? I fought back a hysterical chuckle that threatened to break free. Well, except Husk. He didn't even want to be around me, it seemed. But I couldn't stop thinking about him and how, as crazy as I sounded, I wanted him to like me too.

No, I shouldn't expect more than I already had. I was living the life in Las Vegas with three gorgeous guys in a penthouse suite that had everything I could ever want. I settled deeper into the covers. Both Sky and Winter were passed out and my eyelids drifted closed, too. My life was perfect now. I told myself I didn't need anything else…

ABOUT ARYA KARIN

Arya Karin lives in the south and writes steamy romance and action.

Besides being crazy about reading and obsessed with all things romance, she likes to dance, sing, and spend time with her family.

Want to know more about Arya? Click here to go to her website- https://autho-raryakarin.blogspot.com/

Or sign up for her newsletter: http://eepurl.com/c7lTtr

Sarwah Creed is the Queen of comedy, the Empress of reverse harem, and the Mistress of jaw-dropping twists.

When she's not busy writing her Reverse Harem books that will leave you feeling hot and steamy, then you'll find her in the gym, running, or playing tennis with her kids.

Sarwah's books are available in English, German, Dutch, Spanish, French, and Italian.

She has a sweet tooth and can easily be bribed with chocolate and cupcakes.

If you're a new reader to Sarwah, don't hesitate to sign up for her newsletter and you'll receive a free book!

When you're reading her books, make sure to have a towel nearby because her stories are so steamy, that you'll need something to cool you down!

All social media links----https://linktr.ee/SarwahCreed

BOOK 2 IS OUT NOW!

Hi lovely,

I hope that you enjoyed book 1. Book 2 is out now.

I've included a sneak preview of book 2.

Happy Reading,

Sarwah & Arya

My mate, Husk, rejected me!

What do I care?

Husk is arrogant, stubborn, and pigheaded, the complete opposite of what I want. I can't mate with a brute like him.

Worse, his rejection is causing a rift between him and his brothers, my other mates. I can never give Husk my heart even if he possesses my body.

Fate is cruel and I don't think I can pay the price.

There's a fine line between love and hate, but with me and Husk, it's a mile-long chasm.

HUSK

The whole damn place smelled of fucking sex. My nose wrinkled in disgust, and I kicked off my boots. At least Fagua had learned to control her magic enough not to bring the place down on top of us. Or maybe my brothers weren't as good as they could be at making her orgasm. I snorted. I could outpace both of them.

Giggles sounded from the kitchen, and I debated skipping dinner and going straight to bed. Though I probably needed to pick up some earplugs to drown out their all-night fucking parties.

My wolf whined within my chest, wanting

her as our mate. Stupid wolf didn't know better.

I ignored him and plodded down the hallway toward the kitchen, grumbling under my breath about horny fucking wolves and their insatiable appetites.

In the kitchen, Fagua dropped balls of chocolate-chip cookie dough onto a greased baking pan while Winter stirred a thick, spicy-smelling pasta sauce. Sky chopped the jalapeno sausage.

"Husk, you're back," Sky said, waving the knife at me. "Where have you been?"

I shrugged. "Around." Anywhere but here and having to see these three making goo-goo eyes at each other all the time. Whoever invented the phrase of a third wheel had to have been in this situation.

Then again, I guess I was the fourth wheel, and every damn day, I felt like I grew further apart from all of them. I went to the fridge and took out the milk, drinking it down in a few gulps.

"Hey, I was going to use that to make french toast in the morning," Fagua said as she slid her tray of cookies into the oven.

"Not to mention having milk for these as well."

"Order more, then." I tossed the carton into the trash can. "I'm going to bed. Try to keep your screaming to a minimum tonight."

"Why don't you lay off her?" Winter growled.

"Fuck you." I wiped my mouth with the back of my hand. "Have you two forgotten she thought of us as unruly monsters?"

Fagua stiffened, her full mouth drawing down into a pouty frown. "I'm sorry, okay? You three were kinda overwhelming at first. But you have to admit your table manners needed an upgrade, not to mention you locked me up."

"Save the bullshit." I clenched my fists. "Does no one remember how she fucking left Sky to die?"

"Give her a break, Husk. She didn't underst—"

"No, I won't," I interrupted Sky, who was trying to make the best of everything. It only wound me up the wrong way, and I knew that one day his blind faith was going to get him in trouble.

"Because of her, you nearly died," I growled,

wondering why I had to remind him. "I was the one who wanted her to come to you. We needed her to save you, and she rejected all of this and treated the bonding as dirt. Now, you're both boning her as if you're on a never-ending honeymoon."

"I-I didn't..." She twisted her hands in her apron. Her face was pale and red spots dotted her cheeks.

My gut clenched at the thought that I was hurting her, but I couldn't make myself apologize. I couldn't forget what she'd done and her prejudice against us when she didn't even know us.

Sky rolled his hands into fists. "We've been over this," he said in a cool voice.

"Save it." I lifted my chin, and the muscle in my jaw twitched.

"Why do you have to be so fucking hard on her?" Winter slapped the wooden spoon down on the counter. "If you could try to make this work..."

"She's got you both by the dicks," I snarled. "What the fuck would you know about how to make this work? All you do is listen to her and crawl up her ass every chance you get—even if it means your brother is hungry as hell." I didn't give a shit anymore. "Fuck the three of you. I'm out."

Not listening to their protests, I stormed into the living room and snatched my boots.

I shoved my feet inside and was in the elevator before any of them came out of the kitchen.

There was no way I'd stay in this house with those three. I'd never bond with another werewolf. Ever. And they could forget about my making her my mate. A half-breed? Not a fucking chance.

I slammed the elevator door and rode it down.

I was fed up with all their bullshit. Fagua created a wedge between us and neither of my brothers could see it.

The elevator door dinged open and I stepped out into the lobby. One of the poker table hosts ran up to me, but I waved him off. Let Winter or Sky deal with whatever unruly customers we had. I was done.

I strode toward the exit.

"Husk, wait." Fagua followed behind me as she teetered on her high-heeled sandals that weren't strapped in the back, making her legs look even longer as she walked on the balls of her feet.

"No. I've had it." I pushed the door open and winced at her close proximity.

She grabbed my arm and I jerked it away. "You can't leave."

"Watch me." I stomped toward my bike.

"I'll go with you." She hurried after me, her heels clicking on the sidewalk.

I stopped, my hands clenched at my sides. "You'll do no such thing."

"I don't like this." She glanced back. "It feels wrong to have you leave."

Yeah, and it didn't feel right with my brothers having her either.

"Go back upstairs to my brothers. Don't make me tie you up and hand-deliver you."

She clamped her mouth shut, her face coloring, but as I moved away from her into the cool night, I assumed she decided to go back to them, seeing as we didn't move in the same direction.

I shoved my hands into my jacket pockets. The stars shone brightly and a chill wind blew against me.

I breathed in the scent of the city. Cars honked while a group of young women dressed in sequins jaywalked across the street, laughing.

Traffic whizzed by as the lights blinked red and green, daring me to cross the street. Didn't matter what time of day or night it was, Vegas was always buzzing with gamblers and tourists.

A gust of wind blew, and I tightened my jacket around me and hiked over to my motor-cycle parked outside in a reserved spot. I climbed on and started the engine, my bike purring underneath me.

I zipped down the street, whizzing past cars like they were standing still, and I didn't bother to look back at her.

Yeah, I was being an ass. My brothers loved her and she was making herself at home. But I couldn't get past it. I hated how she'd waltzed into our home and messed up our private pack.

One thing to ease my anger would be to let my wolf out and run.

The breeze carried a multitude of odors. The usual scents of pollution, sweat, and cooking meat were all there, but there was another scent that made the hairs on the back of my neck stand on end.

Wolf.

And not one I recognized.

Shit. I pulled the bike over to the side and flicked the engine off. It had to be my imagination, right? Some wolves out for a holiday in Vegas, maybe? I pushed some money in the parking meter and headed into the city's park.

I jogged ahead, following the trail, and another smell joined the first.

Two wolves. One male and the other… wolf and a hint of something else that I couldn't place. Yet my gut told me there was something wrong with these two being so close.

I picked up the pace, a snarl building in my throat. This was our territory. No other wolves were allowed here without first clearing it with one of us. Or had my brothers forgotten to mention they'd given permission?

No. I shook my head. No, they would have told me even if it had to be in a text.

The trail shifted to Las Vegas's Hidden Forest, and I increased my pace to a run. What the fucking hell were they doing so close to us and not gambling?

Hunting on another's land was taboo, and I know neither of my brothers would've allowed this, no matter who had come to visit.

I hopped over the fence and crouched in the shadows, following their scent.

The moon was hidden behind thick clouds, the air still.

I pushed forward until the scents vanished. Whirling in a circle, I backtracked only to discover the trail ended here in the middle of the fucking forest. Fuck! I'd been too distracted—my anger clouding my judgment—that I had raced after shadows. How had I lost them?

I gave a hard sniff, the trees giving off a sweet scent. Something sour floated on the wind. Blood. A fresh kill of a rabbit lay at the base of a thick tree, half-eaten, both odd wolf scents all over it. Why would they leave this here?

An owl hooted nearby, followed by the distant screech of a bat, and I froze.

Fagua.

My hackles rose. Whoever these wolves were, they'd led me out here on purpose. Fagua and my brothers were in danger.

My wolf clawed at my ribcage to be let out,

but I needed to keep my human form to get back into the casino and up to the suite.

I raced back with my heart in my throat and feeling like I couldn't take deep enough breaths.

I pulled myself together enough to sprint back to my bike. I took off through the trees, running faster than I ever had before. My chest tightened and my breathing was ragged and shallow. A bitter taste curled up my throat.

Whoever was after Fagua and my brothers wanted me out of the way, and I'd stupidly walked right into their trap. My heart raced and my head throbbed. Rage built inside me and I bared my fangs.

Oh God, please don't let me be too late.

My boots pounded across the marble floor of the casino and I didn't even bother with the elevator. I tore through the door to the stairs and took them three at a time with my long strides. My blood pounded in my ears. My breath burned in my chest.

I reached the penthouse level and slammed a fist into the door.

"Fagua," I yelled. The scents of wolves and wrongness choked me.

Muffled shouts sounded from inside along with a growl.

"Sky! Winter!"

I kicked the door in. It almost flew off its hinges at my strength, though it missed a man's face by inches. He greeted me with a deep-throated growl meant to intimidate, but fear flickered across his eyes when he saw who had come charging through the door at him full force like a freight train.

I growled, low and deadly. The man, shirtless with pants, but barefoot, rose to his feet and advanced on me, eyes flashing yellow, teeth bared in fury.

He stared at me, this stranger who appeared out of nowhere.

I didn't waste time with a greeting. I kicked hard into his side with a loud crack that sent him rolling across the floor. I took my time, moving toward him because I assumed he was out of it.

I was wrong because the next thing I knew, he charged toward me.

I met him in the middle and slammed my knee into his gut. He folded over me and I elbowed him in the side of his head, snapping his neck back.

I turned to him, but he was ready for me. He backhanded me across the face. I stumbled but came up with an uppercut that clicked his teeth together.

His eyes rolled up in the back of his head and he slumped to the floor.

I spun and a wolf stared me down.

Where the fuck did the wolf come from?

The wolf was huge, its shoulder was level with my hip and its eyes were solid black.

The wolf looked surprised for a second, then stalked toward me. I rushed in and drove my foot into his side because I didn't have time to change to my wolf form.

It whimpered a growl, snapping at me. I slammed him into the wall, feeling his ribs crack under my palm, and he let out a piercing wail.

Another wolf charged me and I bent low, snatching the first wolf up by the throat and threw it at the other. The half-wolf, half-man growled as it crashed into the other. There was no sign of Fagua or my brothers.

Three more wolves joined in the fight.

Powerful jaws tore into my leg. I held back a yell and kicked him off, then lunged at the next one.

My nails raked into his back and I reeled backward, a snarl ripping from my throat.

Another wolf leapt at me. I dodged and sliced my claws across his throat as I started to shift while fighting them. I couldn't do it fully; I needed every muscle in my body to do that, and I didn't have time to concentrate on it. Not when I had to fight these fucking wolves that seemed to spring up in every corner of my damn house!

Fucking spawn of the devil.

I lunged at the first wolf again. He twisted as I went for his throat and managed to get his teeth into my side.

I roared in pain as he shook his head. I clawed his muzzle. He let me go and I throat-punched him. He crumbled, choking on blood and pain.

Another wolf chomped down on my arm.

I snarled and shoved my claws into his eye sockets. The wolf yelped and stumbled a few feet back, cowering.

I lunged at him again, but something wrapped around my waist and yanked me back.

I kicked at whatever restrained me. A sickening crunch sounded and I grinned.

Wolves circled me, yet their scent of fear clogged my throat.

Had Fagua been hurt? My heart twisted in my chest and I had to push aside the pain and dread. If one hair on her head was damaged, each of these bastards was going to pay in blood.

My wolf thumped in my chest, but I was going to rip these fuckers apart with my half-transformed hands.

I swung around, claws extended. A wolf snapped at my leg.

I grabbed its forearm and twisted it. A sickening crunch sounded as the shoulder popped out of the socket.

It screamed in pain and I threw it at the other wolves. Three went down from the impact and two were trampled as the wolves scrambled to get away from me.

I roared and charged at the wolves closest to me. I knocked them down one by one, my fist pounding into their flesh.

A sharp, blinding pain ripped through my shoulder.

A pained howl erupted from my throat. My fingers dug into the wolf's neck as I fell to the floor. I turned and drove my fist into its stomach. It growled but scurried away from me. I laid on the carpet as spots danced in my vision. Shit! Not now. I couldn't fucking pass out here in the middle of a fight. Stupid curse needed a kick up its ass.

The wolves closed in on me.

Baring my teeth, I pushed up into a crouch, ready to spring forward.

"Stop," Fagua shouted.

The wolves jerked their gazes from me and looked to their left.

Fagua stepped past the wolves. Her eyes flashed red and her hands were curling and uncurling at her sides. I could have sworn I saw wisps of magic flare around her.

"Not one fucking step closer, or I'll rip your

spines out and make you eat them," she warned.

Most of the wolves took a step away, but two didn't. My heart throbbed in my chest.

The wolves crept closer to her.

I leaped at them, but she threw her hands up, her magic barreling into them and knocking them to the ground. But they weren't giving up. I punched and kicked all who dared come too close to her, putting myself between her and the wolves. Pain laced through me from my injury, but I didn't stop. I wouldn't stop until she was safe.

Blood and fists flew. Rage bubbled up in my chest until all the wolves raced out the door.

Footsteps sounded behind me from the bedroom.

I swung around, claws extended, and ended up facing a young woman.

Her eyes were sharp and blue as she looked at me with a mixture of disbelief and fear.

A wolf bitch.

Had she been with Fagua and hurt her? I grabbed her by the throat and shoved her against the wall. I pressed my forearm against her neck, cutting off her air. "Who the fuck are you? You've got three seconds to tell me or you die along with your wolf pups here."

Before I could do anything else, Fagua punched my shoulder.

"I won't let you hurt her!" Fagua barked, punching my shoulder again. Her hand was small, but her punches stung. I froze, feeling the heat of her anger.

I stopped. My chest ached at the horror in Fagua's gaze. She thought I was going to kill a female?

I stared down at the woman panting in front of me. Tears glistened in her eyes. She smelled of wolf and something else, but I couldn't place it. It felt like something dead, but that wasn't possible.

Shame and guilt pooled in my gut. I let her go, taking a step back.

The woman let out a gasp, her hands flying to her chest, and she leaned against the wall like it was the only thing supporting her.

"It will be all right," Fagua said. "Don't be afraid. We mean you no harm."

"What the fuck is going on?" I asked, the adrenaline from the fight still surging through me. "Where are Sky and Winter?"

"They went looking for you." Fagua crossed her arms over her chest. She was barefoot and only wore a button-down shirt that hit her knees. Her shirt gaped open, showing off a flat, smooth belly and the creamy color of her breasts. My cock jerked at the sight.

"And they left you here unprotected?"

"I can take care of myself."

She raised her chin in defiance, and I had the sudden urge to put my mouth on hers, to taste it, to kiss away whatever was pissing her off so much.

"Right. You'd have been wolf mincemeat if I hadn't shown up." When I saw my brothers again, I was going to punch them both for abandoning her. They're all about her being their mate.

I wanted her too, but I wouldn't share her.

My lips twisted at that thought. How the hell was I supposed to share her with my brothers?

She's Fagua. She's not just some girl who wants to be kissed.

I clenched my fists to keep from putting my hands all over her, from stroking that soft-looking skin until she moaned and writhed beneath me.

"You're not going to hurt me?" the woman asked, giving me a wary glance.

I frowned, my wolf snarling in my chest. "Who are you? And what the fuck are you doing here?"

She raised her chin. "My name is Mayia. I was sent here to speak with you."

I stepped in front of Fagua, putting myself between her and the girl. "About what?"

"I'll speak to Fagua alone."

"I'm not going anywhere," I said.

I glared at the girl with her pale skin and dark eyes with matching hair. I didn't like her scent. Dead-like. There was only one creature who smelled like that—a fucking vampire. I'd only been in the presence of one and then I'd ripped him to death.

Curiosity got the better of me. I wanted to hear what she had to say, so I allowed her time to speak. "You have five minutes."

She nodded and took a deep breath, probably waiting for me to leave them alone. That wasn't what I agreed to. I said she had five minutes, but that wouldn't be alone with Fagua. "I'm the mate to the Alpha of the Stone Pack."

My eyes narrowed, thinking she couldn't be telling the truth. No way was she a wolf. "You don't smell like a wolf. Not completely."

"I'm a wolf and…" Mayia hesitated, and her gaze flickered to Fagua before returning to me.

She closed her eyes and whispered, "A vampire."

My eyes narrowed. As I'd suspected, she was a vampire, but only half. Still, it made no sense as to why she was even here.

"What the fuck?" I blurted because wolves hated vamps more than witches. And vampires loved to kill as many of us as they could. How the hell had two arch-enemies mated?

"Listen, I don't have time to explain." She paled. "Fagua, your father isn't happy you left."

How the hell did she know this? Shit, I couldn't take it anymore. Not only had they broken in, but now they were talking as if we knew each other and we were all friends, and trying to advise Fagua about her dad.

"I can take him if he wants to challenge me or my brothers," I said proudly, though I was lying, but she didn't know me well enough to know it was far from the truth. I didn't have the strength to fight more than five wolves, let alone a whole army. Heat licked at my shoulders and a low growl rumbled in my chest.

"No." Fagua cleared her throat, panic in her eyes. "He's alpha and I've seen him tear apart others, even wolves bigger and stronger than him." The way Fagua's lips trembled and her eyes widened told me she saw the truth in Mayia's words.

"He's brutal." Mayia shuddered.

"I won't let that happen," I said, my fists curling at my sides. I'd kill anyone who tried to hurt her. Not even the gods could stop me.

"He would never hurt his own daughter," Mayia said, and I watched her bare her teeth. "But he won't hesitate to hurt you or your brothers."

My gaze narrowed. "Why should I believe you? Why should I believe any of this?"

"Because," Mayia said. "He will hurt those she cares about if she doesn't come back. Now."

My gut clenched. "Why does he need Fagua?"

"He wants to mate her to the highest bidder." Mayia's tone wavered and she played with a lock of her dark hair. "And he won't take no for an answer."

"He'll send more wolves after us." Fagua's voice was tight.

Mayia nodded.

"Do you believe her?" I asked Fagua. No way did I trust Mayia or these wolves that had attacked me.

"Not sure." She rubbed her arms.

"You've had your five minutes, you can go now." My words were directed at Mayia. I thought she would cause trouble and say more than she'd already said, but she bowed her head and then Fagua walked with her to the elevator, showing her the way out.

It was as if Fagua could read my mind as she directed out, even if it was ironic that Mayia had gotten in somehow, but she'd needed to be led out.

Still, I waited in the hallway with my arms crossed until Mayia left and Fagua walked back into the suite.

My head pounded and damn spots appeared in my vision. "I'm getting a beer. You want anything?"

I could have asked her how things went

with Mayia, but one thing about Fagua and me was that we didn't do small talk. In fact we didn't really talk at all, until now.

"I'll take one, thanks."

I went into the kitchen and opened the fridge. My vision wavered. I gripped the refrigerator door to keep from stumbling. I shut my eyes against the dizziness.

My teeth clenched.

I breathed deeply through my nose to cool the fire in my blood. To ease the desire of having Fagua in my arms, in my bed. My curse was tearing me apart. I wanted to be free of this pain, these cravings.

Stupid-ass wolf.

Just another part of being a werewolf, and he was throwing a fit. My body trembled and I crashed to the floor. Darkness burst behind my eyes.

Fuck, fuck, fuck!

I knew what this was. My wolf—my soul— ripping me apart because I hadn't mated with Fagua yet. I would die if I didn't mate with her, but how could I share her? The idea sent rage coiling in my gut.

Now what the hell was I going to do?